AMBUSH AT ANTLERS SPRING

AMBUSH AT JAYTI EKS SPRING

AMBUSH AT ANTLERS SPRING

Will Cook

Chivers Press • G.K. Hall & Co.
Bath, Avon, England   Thorndike, Maine USA

This Large Print edition is published by Chivers Press, England, and by G.K. Hall & Co., USA.

Published in 1996 in the U.K. by arrangement with the author's estate.

Published in 1996 in the U.S. by arrangement with Golden West Literary Agency.

U.K. Hardcover ISBN 0–7451–4828–X (Chivers Large Print)
U.K. Softcover   ISBN 0–7451–4840–9 (Camden Large Print)
U.S. Softcover   ISBN 0–7838–1737–1 (Nightingale Collection Edition)

The text of this Large Print edition is unabridged.
Other aspects of the book may vary from the original edition.

Set in 16 pt. New Times Roman.

Printed in Great Britain on acid-free paper.

British Library Cataloguing in Publication Data available

Library of Congress Cataloging-in-Publication Data

Cook, Will.
    Ambush at Antlers Spring / Will Cook.
       p.   cm.
LT-W   ISBN 0–7838–1737–1 (lg. print : sc)
    1. Large type books.   I. Title.
    [PS3553.O5547A43   1996]
    813′.54—dc20

                                        96–10406

CHAPTER ONE

All that long afternoon they were working down from the high country, slowed by the rain that had turned the trails to mud, and the rock surface to a treacherous slime. Each cutbank was a new danger to horses and men. Trooper McGee nearly drowned in Fish Creek, normally a dry wash, now swollen from bank to bank with red muddy water.

Nineteen men were all that was left of C Company—Sergeant T. C. Manlove temporarily in command. Their officer lay in the hills behind them, along with six enlisted men who had died of wounds on the way back. Manlove's thoughts were gloomy as he rode at the head of the column.

The mounted men slogged along under the dismal gray sky. There was no hurry now. This was a retreat. A full company had ridden out from Antlers Spring, and nineteen survivors were riding back.

That was how it was when you fought Apaches. You never saw them till a fraction of a second before the firing began. A yell, a brown figure popping up, and then all hell broke loose around you; this was Manlove's thought as he jogged along.

Even in his flowing poncho Manlove was short, squat and broad as an oak stump. He

1

was thirty-eight years old, and for twenty-four of those years he had been in the Army. He had begun as a drummer boy with Hood, and later, when he became a man, had taken up the saber and worn the cavalry yellow on his trouser leg.

Reaching far back into memory, Manlove could recall his father, a peace-loving man with a fertile wife who bred yearly. Manlove had had eleven brothers and sisters, and now it was only with an effort that he could call their names to mind. Manlove had been the third son, and the third to go, for it was his father's way to put the boys out at fourteen. The land was poor, and as each newborn came along, regular as the spring thaw, an older, hungrier child had to go.

Tim Manlove's signature on his first enlistment papers had been a scrawled X, and for six years he had signed the payroll that way. Then a cranky mule had broken both his legs, and the surgeon had taken pity on him and taught him his ABCs. It was a door opening on a new world to Manlove. He learned to read the regulations and write reports; he learned surveying, and accounting. His eye for detail, along with a dogged devotion to duty, put the chevrons on his sleeves one after another until he wore the diamond-in-the-vee, the rank of top soldier.

Now and then Manlove turned in the saddle and looked behind, to see if anyone had fallen out. Only a few of the men were wounded, none of them seriously. But the rain had turned the footing dangerous, and every dry wash was a roaring river. Tomorrow, under the baking sun, the land would dry and crack. That was the climate in Arizona, either bone dry or sopping wet.

Manlove worked his men down to the lower, timbered levels before he halted the column. They took what little shelter the dripping trees afforded. Corporal Kincaid came forward when Manlove motioned.

Wiping the water from his face, Manlove asked, 'How are they making it?' There was concern in his deep voice, a regret that he had to make wounded men ride at all. 'Do they want another three hours of this?'

'Hell, you're the boss, Tim,' Kincaid answered. He was almost a runt, wire-thin, a mere hundred and thirty pounds of soldier, but he was hard. His face was burned to the consistency of leather by the sun, weathered like an old boot left out too long. His hands were rough and heavily calloused, and the knuckles had all been broken at one time or another.

Manlove shook his heavy head. He took off his hat. His hair, thick and damp, gave off a strong, unwashed odor. 'After what they've been through, they've got a say. Hell, I'm no damned Pointer.'

'Another ten miles means dry bunks,' Kincaid said. 'They all want that. And the two

3

wounded need the surgeon. Svensen's still got lead in him.'

'All right,' Manlove said wearily. 'We'll finish it out, but the old man's going to scream. I guess we should have brought Lieutenant Bestor back with us.'

'Let the old man go back and get him,' Kincaid said and went back to his section.

Manlove got his troopers mounted and moving again. They were reluctant to leave the shelter of the trees, and he did not blame them; some sit-down and a fire would have been welcome.

The fight was still fresh and painful in his mind. Diablito had caught them moving along the length of a narrow canyon. Apache fashion, he had opened fire after a single scream of warning. The first volley had dropped Lieutenant Bestor and Trooper Halloran. The column had wheeled to pull back, only to run into more Apaches who hacked them to pieces. Lieutenant Bestor's foot had caught in a stirrup and he had been dragged for nearly a mile.

When it was over, all the survivors could do was gather up the guns and ammunition to keep them out of Apache hands, pull back and lick their wounds.

There was something grimly ironic about this campaign, Tim Manlove thought, for down at Camp Bowie and Camp Apache, General George Crook was making police out of the Apaches, taming them to eat out of his hand. This political maneuvering was an aftermath of the fighting; the Army had to do something to warrant Congressional appropriations and avoid a cutback in strength.

So General Crook preached peace and education for the Apaches, and the only holdout was Diablito—more myth than man, a foxy old renegade who had been leaving a trail of blood behind him for thirty years.

The great ones were gone: Mangus Colorado, Cuchillo Negro; even the great Geronimo had surrendered. All was peace in Apacheria, except for this ghost, Diablito, who had remained hidden from the white man's eyes for twenty years.

Diablito was a symbol of Apache anger and Apache revenge. His name was whispered with awe among the six thousand Apaches. He was a stalker in the shadows, a focal point for rebellion. Diablito was the one man who stood in the way of peace, and Crook wanted him killed or captured at any cost.

The cost would be heavy, Manlove thought. In six months they had lost more men than the fort could afford. They had worn out butts and saddles and horses, and had not even found Diablito's camp.

Diablito had been raiding unchecked for nearly the span of Manlove's life, and had gone almost unnoticed, for the old fox covered his trail so well that Geronimo or some other Apache usually got the blame. Only now, when there was peace in Apacheria, was Diablito's activity evident.

The isolated ranchers watched the horizon anxiously, but in vain; Diablito always struck without warning, vanished afterward without sign into his mountain stronghold. The cavalry always pursued him but never caught up.

Manlove brought his men home well after dark. Their post was an abandoned stage relay station. They had erected temporary barracks, enlarged the corral to accommodate the horses, put up a stockade wall. No one had ever troubled to give the place an official name; they called it the Antlers Spring Station and let it go at that. Besides, General Crook was not anxious to acknowledge it as an active military post, for that meant admitting that a hostile situation existed, one the Army could not control.

The station lay on the flats, in the middle of a broad valley where the sun could fry it every day and the desert winds roared through, bringing sand and tumbleweeds and misery. Hardly a day passed that someone did not kill a rattlesnake in the yard or dump a scorpion out of his boot.

When Manlove rode in with his men, Captain George Dane came out to meet him. A glance was enough to tell Dane that Bestor was gone.

In a bleak voice, he said, 'Come into the office, Sergeant, as soon as you dismiss the men.' Then he turned and stood under the porch to keep out of the rain. Lamplight from the windows outlined him—a tall, lean man who stood uncompromisingly straight, as though he were trying hard to bear up under a difficult duty.

Corporal Kincaid took charge of the detail while Manlove followed Dane into the office. Dane poured a glass of whiskey and pushed it across his desk.

'That ought to put some heat back in you,' he said. 'Sit down. Bestor's dead?'

'Yes, sir.'

'A dirty business,' Dane said wearily. He stroked his dense mustache, pulled at his lip. 'I can't ask Crook for another officer. The man must think I'm a bungling incompetent, continually losing men, continually asking for replacements.'

'Maybe Crook ought to come out here and chase Diablito himself,' Manlove said. He leaned back in the chair and folded his thick hands. 'Captain, I've served sixteen years with you. Can I speak my mind?'

'If it will help, I want to hear it,' Dane said.

'Well, sir, I don't think the cavalry's going to whip Diablito. Captain, we ride into those mountains loaded down with equipment, jingling like a team of circus horses. Hell, on a still day you can hear us coming for three

7

miles.'

'I didn't write the regulations,' Dane said. 'What are you leading up to?'

'Just this, sir.' Manlove searched for his tobacco sack and found it a wet ruin. Dane immediately offered a cigar, which was what Manlove had wanted in the first place.

'We got the hell whipped out of us today, sir, and I'm getting tired of that. I've been in and out of those mountains, chasing that damned ghost for seven years. Out of it all, some sense is coming.' Manlove got up and stepped over to Dane's wall map. 'The first raid he pulled in this district was at the Kingsley place fifty miles north. He killed the old man, three boys, the old woman, and took the girl. She was seventeen or eighteen at the time, and has never been seen since. Then there was the Pillsbury place—the men killed, a girl taken.'

'But that was almost a year later,' Dane said.

'Right,' Manlove said. 'But let me finish. The Garner place was next, then Randall's, and Carter's. No horses taken, and all the men and older women killed, the girls taken. None of them were ever heard of again.' He came back and sat down. 'Captain, how old do you think Diablito is?'

'Sixty, or thereabout.'

'I think the same myself,' Manlove said. 'Now here's a man, sixty, living wild. He knows he's a ghost, a legend, but he also knows he's a man. He'll die, and the legend will die with him.

8

He's an old man with the seed of life still in his loins, and I add it up to one thing—he's raiding for a woman who'll bear him a son.'

George Dane leaned slowly forward and a light came into his eyes. 'Sergeant, you're blowing a strong, clear call. Keep talking.'

'He's taken five women, and none of them have given him what he wants, a son to carry on the legend. He's killed the girls, one by one, and now he's hunting for another. Captain, in this last year I've seen a thousand tracks. I've cut one trail after another in the rimrock country, like some big pattern laid out that's just beginning to show clear. Captain, there's only three young girls worth Diablito's bothering with within fifty miles. The two Johnson girls, and Marge Kearn. Where they are is where Diablito will raid next. He's got to.'

Captain Dane sat motionless for a moment, then slapped his hand on the desk. 'Damn it, I think you've hit on the truth of it. Now that you spell it out, I realize that something like this has been floating around in the back of my mind for a long time. But what's the answer? Guard the two ranches? We can't spare the men. Bringing their women here for safety is impossible—these civilians would suspect any reason we gave. What do you propose?'

'To get that Apache ghost before he takes one more woman to his blanket.'

'We've tried that already, a time or two,'

9

Dane said wryly.

'Captain, I'd like to go into Diablito's country in my own way.'

'How's that?'

'I'll pick four men. We'll ride unshod ponies, carry only rifles and ammunition and a little dried meat. No regulation equipment, sir. We'll live like Apaches and hunt them out on their own terms.'

'You'd never make it,' Dane said flatly. 'For one thing, you're not Apaches—they can smell each other's thoughts.'

Manlove smiled. 'I think some of us have learned the stink. We know the country, and we only risk five men. Isn't it worth the gamble?'

'I don't want to lose five more men,' George Dane said. He looked steadily at Manlove. 'Whom would you take?'

'Bob Kincaid, if he'd go. And Sergeant Brady and Corporal Riley.'

'That makes four.'

'And you, Captain.'

'Me?' George Dane laughed. 'Now I know you're crazy. Crook would accuse me of deserting my command.'

'You've got Lieutenant Meeker left,' Manlove pointed out. 'Would you rather I took him?'

'No, no,' Dane said quickly. 'Meeker's too young, too green.' He got up and began to pace back and forth. He turned and looked at

10

Manlove. 'Can five of us do it?'

'Fighting the Apache way, yes.'

Dane gnawed on his cigar. 'I don't believe it, Sergeant. We wouldn't last thirty days.'

'Thirty days may be all we need,' Manlove said. 'With Meeker here to keep up the patrol action, Diablito might be kept busy watching him and miss us. Meeker wouldn't have to penetrate far, sir.'

'That's true. Can you get Brady and Kincaid to volunteer? And who was the other one?'

'Riley, sir.'

'Yes, Riley. Will they go?'

'I think so. They all hate Apaches and know the country. Riley's wife was taken nine years ago, sir. Never heard of since.'

'Yes, I recall that now. All right, Sergeant, you've made yourself a deal. Have you decided what you'll need?'

'I might be able to buy the unshod ponies from Sam Kearn, sir.'

'I'll give you some army scrip,' Dane said.

Manlove smiled. 'Better make it gold, Captain. Since young Kearn got court-martialed, the old man thinks poorly of the Army. And I'd like to see us armed with Winchesters, Captain. These trap-door Springfields are fine for slow fire, but—'

'I'll send Meeker into Lordsburg,' Dane said. He paused, thinking. 'We'll need clothes. Sergeant, you get the volunteers and I'll make up a list. We'll go over it later to see if I've left anything out.' He took a few cigars from his humidor and gave them to Manlove. 'This may help with the volunteering.'

'A bottle wouldn't hurt either, Captain.'

'I suppose it wouldn't,' Dane said, and produced one from his clothes chest.

With the cigars and the bottle of whiskey, Manlove walked to his quarters, a converted tack shed near the barn. He shared it with three other noncommissioned officers.

Sergeant Brady was taking a bath when Manlove came in. He glanced up alertly. 'Is that a bottle of whiskey?'

'It is. The captain's own private stock. Have a cigar.'

Bob Kincaid said from his bunk, 'I have a feeling we're all about to volunteer for something, or we'll never see the cork drawn.'

Brady stood up and began to dry himself. He was tall, heavily muscled. 'I've been in the Army seventeen years, and the only way I've ever got a drink between paydays was to volunteer for something.' He paused to light his cigar. 'How did the old man take the losses?'

'Grim around the mouth,' Manlove said. 'How many have taken a bath in that water?'

'I did,' Brady said. 'Why?'

'Then I guess it's not too dirty to use.' Manlove began to undress. His chest was like a keg; his shoulders and back were humped with muscle. He sat down in the tub and sighed. 'I've been wet for ten hours, but this water feels different.'

Dan Riley spoke up for the first time. 'When you going to uncork the whiskey?'

'We'll celebrate in a minute.'

Kincaid frowned. 'Celebrate what?'

'Us going after Diablito. Five of us, with Winchesters and unshod ponies.' He looked at their attentive faces. 'It'll be cold camps and raw rattlesnake meat. We'll cut them to pieces, Apache style.'

Brady said, 'There's four of us here. Who's the fifth?'

'Captain Dane.'

There was a pause. 'He ain't a bad officer,' Riley said. 'Of course I've only been with him nine years and I don't know him too well.' He sighed and reached for the bottle. He held it with exaggerated care. 'I know enough about Apaches to be one. And I know how to kill 'em, too. Can I uncork this now?'

Manlove asked, 'Are you all in?'

'Sure we're in,' Brady said. 'I'll get the cups.'

Riley looked hard at Manlove. 'That damned Apache can be like a sickness to a man, getting so that's all he thinks about. When he's gone we're all going to feel a little lost.'

'I won't feel that way,' Tim Manlove said. 'I'm going to retire. Half pay's good enough for me. I'm going to get me a house and build a fence around it and paint it white. Maybe I'll

13

open up a store in Lordsburg. I'm going to have what I never had, a home of my own.' He got out of the tub, began to dress.

'Hell,' Brady said, 'you're going to die in the Army and that's all there is to it.'

'I know that too,' Manlove said softly. 'But there's no hurt in thinking about things.'

CHAPTER TWO

This was a far corner of Arizona Territory, a lonesome, desolate country. The land lay in broad stretches of rolling desert and angry upthrustings of rock, reaching into the clouds at times—a stronghold of Gila monsters and rattlesnakes and Apaches.

Within sixty miles there was one town, Lordsburg; one Army post, Antlers Spring; four ranches, far apart; and one Apache camp, Diablito's, restless and moving as the wind. The rest was heat and horizons so far away that the eyes ached to look at them.

Manlove had gold in his pocket. He and Ike Brady left Antlers Spring before dawn and cut out across the broad valley. Their destination lay near the mountains to the north, where Sam Kearn and his son worked hard at ranching. Kearn had a good well and was backed against a river that ran most of the time, but sleeping with one eye open the way he

14

had to, he could not make any real progress against the land. Still, Kearn fared better than most, because he was a shrewd man. He bred some horses which he sold to the Army; they paid his overhead in a good year and cut his losses on cattle in a bad year.

Manlove and Brady stopped at noon for cold meat and biscuits, then rode on. During the latter part of the afternoon they could make out Kearn's buildings and the trees around his spring.

The sun was going down when they reached the place. All the buildings were adobe, with three-foot walls. The windows were too small for a man to pass through. The walls were deeply pocked by bullets, for Kearn had been under attack by Indians many times.

There was no sign of life until Manlove and Brady rode into the yard, close enough to be recognized.

Then Kearn opened the massive door and stepped out, a .45–75 Winchester in the crook of his arm. He watched in silence while Manlove and Brady dismounted.

'You're a careful man,' Brady said.

Sam Kearn answered, 'Last month an Apache came on the place wearing dirty-shirt blue.' He jerked his thumb in the direction of the barn. 'He's buried under the manure pile. I got the clothes inside.' He stared at Tim Manlove. 'One Kearn was accused of stealing government property, and that's one too many

15

for me.'

'Now, don't start that,' Manlove said with some irritation.

'All right, I won't. What do you want on my place?'

'Horses,' Manlove said. 'I know Howard brought back a bunch from Utah last month.'

Sam Kearn shook his head. 'All Indian ponies. No cavalry stock there.' He grinned mirthlessly. 'Diablito steal some of your horses?'

'No,' Manlove said. 'I want Indian ponies. Unshod.'

Kearn rubbed his chin. 'Come in. I may have what you want.'

Manlove and Brady went into the parlor. The room was airless and hot. Dust lay on the furniture, not because Kearn's house was badly kept but because it was impossible to keep dust off.

'I'll have Marge bring some coffee,' Kearn said, and left the room.

Ike Brady said, 'Well, he seems well-spoken enough.'

'Don't let it fool you,' Manlove told him.

Kearn came in again and sat down. 'It'll be a few minutes,' he said. 'When did the Army start buying unshod ponies?' His glance touched Brady, but settled on Manlove. He knew enough of the Army to know that senior rank would answer.

'We're going Apache hunting,' said

16

Manlove. 'And we don't want to advertise the fact to the wrong people.'

Kearn's lined face pulled into a grimace. 'Luck to you.'

He turned his head as a man's footsteps came through the kitchen toward the parlor.

Howard Kearn stopped in the doorway when he saw Manlove. He looked at his father, indicating Manlove with a small gesture. 'I thought you told him not to come back.'

Howard was a big man, inclined to quick temper. There had been bad blood between him and Manlove ever since Howard had been kicked out of the Army.

'Sit down and cool off,' Kearn said. 'I'd listen to the devil himself if he had anything to say.'

Howard hesitated, then flopped into a chair. 'What's the matter, Tim? Afraid to come alone?'

'Scared to death,' Tim Manlove said.

'All right now, damn it, he came to buy horses.' Kearn scowled at his son. 'I told you last year to settle your trouble in Lordsburg, if it's ever going to be settled.' He pawed his mouth out of shape, then reached for his tobacco. 'How many ponies do you want, Manlove?'

'Ten, if I can pick them.'

'You'll pay top price for the best,' Kearn said. 'I won't give them away.'

'I didn't come here to steal them,' Manlove

17

said.

Howard Kearn reared out of his chair. His father put out a hand to push him back. 'I'm sure that was only a manner of speaking. Isn't that so, Manlove?'

'As it happened, it was a manner of speaking,' Manlove said. 'But I'm not going to walk on eggs around him. Sam, he stole three Army horses and sold them. If a man had done that to you, you'd have hung him. But being as it was Army business, he got a year and the boot. Now, I'm not going to walk around that—here, or anyplace else.'

'I guess we'd better drop the matter, then,' Sam Kearn grumbled.

'Suppose I don't want to drop it?' Howard asked.

Manlove stared at him. 'Friend, it don't matter a damn to me, either way.'

Silence fell, broken as Marge Kearn came in with a coffee pot and cups on a tray. She was tall and big-boned for a girl. The glance she gave Tim Manlove was long and searching.

Marge said, 'There's some pie left over from yesterday if anyone wants it.'

'I don't,' Sam Kearn said, managing to suggest that no one else did either.

'Marge, I never could resist your pie,' Manlove said, ignoring frowns from father and son. He got up, took the tray out of her hands and put it on a table. 'I think I'll supervise the cut of this. I don't want to be a hog. Neither do

18

I want to get too small a slice.'

'I thought you came here to talk about horses,' Howard said with a scowl.

'We'll talk about them,' Manlove went back into the kitchen with Marge.

When she was certain no one could overhear, she faced him and said, 'Tim, you just like to wave a red flag in front of Pa's nose, don't you?' Her eyes were dark with concern. 'What did you really come here for?'

'Horses,' he said. 'And to see you. I wanted to find out if you really hated me.'

'I never hated you. But it was you that forced me to make a choice, Tim. You wanted all or nothing.'

He shrugged. 'That's the truth, I did.' He took her hand and she did not resist. 'I've never gambled away my pay, or drunk it up either. For nineteen years now, I've sent forty dollars a month to a bank in Chicago. Do you know what that adds up to? Over nine thousand dollars, plus all that interest. I don't rightly know how much money I have, but it's considerable. Marge, I'd retire tomorrow if you'd go with me.'

She smiled. 'Tim, it wouldn't make any difference to me if you lived from payday to payday. I just don't want to leave bad blood behind.'

'Is that all it is?' he asked. 'You don't figure I'm too old for you?'

She put her hand briefly to his cheek. 'How

can you ask a fool thing like that? Go along with you, Tim Manlove.' She turned away, took a knife and cut the pie.

Manlove accepted the slice she gave him. 'We'll talk again later,' he told her and carried his pie back to the living room.

Sam Kearn said, 'For the time it took, I thought you was baking a new one.' He puffed on his pipe. 'I figure my horses are worth forty dollars a head.'

'More like fifty,' Howard said.

'Now we don't have to rob the Army just because we don't like it,' Sam said. 'Forty dollars is reasonable to me.'

'I take it they're Navaho ponies,' Manlove said.

'They could be,' Howard said. 'What difference does it make?'

'None to me,' said Manlove, 'but it probably does to the buck who lost them.' Howard started out of the chair, and Tim Manlove pointed a finger at him as if it were the barrel of a pistol. 'You've got a bad habit there, and one fine day you're going to pop up and get popped back down a sight faster. If you want to steal Indian ponies, you go right ahead. I'm not asking for any bill of sale. But when a man's business is cleaning out a honey house, he can't complain when folks remark about the odor.'

'Stealin' from an Indian,' Sam Kearn said judiciously, 'ain't really stealin'.' He looked at his son without warmth. 'We intended to use that stock ourselves, Manlove.'

'Who am I doing business with?' Manlove asked. 'You or Howard?'

'You do business with me,' Sam Kearn said flatly. 'I pay my son thirty dollars a month. That's all he's worth. Whatever he gets for those ponies is his, but this is my place and you'll do business with me.' He got out of his chair. 'Let's go look at them.'

Manlove and Kearn climbed to the top rail of the corral and studied the ponies. The tallest was no more than thirteen hands high. Manlove motioned for Brady to shake out a rope and start cutting. Following Manlove's directions Brady made his cast, snubbed the first pony tight and began to examine him.

The ponies Manlove accepted were put in a small holding corral. It was almost dark before they finished and went back to the house.

Inside, Manlove made his offer, two hundred dollars, and had it angrily rejected. They sat down and had a drink of whiskey and Kearn made a counter-offer, three and a half. Good horse trading took time, but Manlove cut it short by offering three hundred, flat and final.

Kearn grumbled, but accepted, and Manlove paid over the money in gold eagles. Kearn passed the coins to his son.

'If we can sleep in the barn,' Manlove said, 'We'll start back before dawn.'

'All right,' Kearn said. 'Will you eat supper

21

with us?'

Howard stood up, got his canvas coat and started for the door.

'Where the hell you goin'?' Kearn asked.

'Lordsburg.'

'There's work to do here.'

'Then I'll do it when I come back.' Howard went out.

'A moody boy,' Kearn said softly. 'Hard to figure.'

He stared at the toes of his worn boots. 'My girl, Marge, she grew up just as gentle as she was when she was a baby. But Howard, he was a hard boy to get along with. Hate is all that boy knows.' Kearn sighed. 'I hoped the Army would knock some sense into him. When the trouble came, I tried to think of Marge. I guess you and her would have been married and had a kid or two by now if all that had never happened. But I had to stand by Howard—you see that, don't you? I'm his pa, and I had to hate the Army a little, too.'

'When are you going to kick him out, Sam? He's twenty-six.'

'I don't kick my kids out,' Kearn said. He sniffed the air. 'Marge is getting supper. You can wash outside at the spring, I guess.'

Manlove found Brady by the barn. They walked to the spring and bathed in the horse trough, with their rifles leaning nearby.

Brady asked, 'Where did Howard go?'

'Lordsburg. That pony money was burning

his pockets pretty bad. He'll be back in a few days, smelling like an old wine barrel, red-eyed and stone broke.'

'I got drunk every payday, my first hitch,' Brady said. 'But I learned better.'

'Some do. Some don't,' Manlove said, and flogged the dust from his clothes before putting them on.

Back in the house, Brady went into the parlor, but Tim Manlove stayed in the hot kitchen. Marge was at the stove, sweat dampening the shoulders and side of her dress.

Manlove said, 'Do you have to work that way?'

She glanced at him. 'It's the way women work, Tim.'

'Not my woman,' he said. 'On hot nights we'd eat cold ham and cheese.'

'And on cold nights?'

He smiled. 'We'd go to bed early.'

Her quick glance was a mixture of shyness and pleasure. He changed the subject. 'Sam told me he killed an Apache dressed as a soldier. They're getting bold, coming in that way. Must be something here they want bad.' He took her arm and turned her to face him. 'Diablito spends a lot of time in the hills, looking at this place. I've studied his sign. He knows you're here. I think that Apache came in for a closer look at you.'

'I try not to think about such things,' she said. She put her hands flat against his chest.

23

'Tim, I'm glad you're staying the night.' She heard her father's step in the hall and drew away. When Kearn came in, she was again at the stove, and Manlove was standing idly near the table.

'Got some good cigars in the parlor,' Kearn said and went back.

'Now that was a hint if I ever heard one,' said Manlove. He started to leave, then thought better of it and swung back. 'How long since I've kissed you, Marge?'

'Too long,' she said and put down the wooden stirring spoon.

He put his arms around her and felt the heat of her, the wet warmth of her lips. They stood that way for a moment, and he thought of the time lost for them.

When they drew apart, she said, 'You'd better go smoke one of Pa's cigars.'

'Trying to get rid of me?'

'I'll see you after the cigar,' she said and gave him a little push.

He went into the parlor and found Brady sitting stiffly in a chair, solemnly puffing one of Kearn's odorous Moonshine Crooks.

Manlove accepted a cigar and a light, then settled into a chair.

Kearn said, 'I hear you've been losing men regular.'

'More than the general likes. But we plan on changing that.'

'Damned if I'd go into them mountains after

24

Diablito,' Kearn said. 'I've stayed out of those hills for twenty years. There's nothing up there I want. Say, I'll get those Army duds the Apache was wearing.'

'No hurry about it,' Manlove said, but Kearn was already rising.

'I'd better, before I forget,' he said and went down the hall.

'He's got a crust on him an inch thick,' said Ike Brady.

'Pretty tough pie, at that,' Manlove said. He looked at Brady and grinned. 'If we could get him to come along, we'd double our chances. He's forgot more Apache savvy than Crook's best scout ever knew.'

CHAPTER THREE

Lieutenant Paul Meeker arrived in Lordsburg just before the stores closed. He made his purchases and had them taken to a hotel room—he planned to stay the night rather than make a long night ride of it or camp on the desert.

This was Meeker's first tour of duty on the frontier. He was a methodical young man who liked planning and detail and hoped some day to earn an appointment to staff. His record was good but not outstanding. His superiors found him dependable but unimaginative.

The hotel room was small and still hot from being closed up all day. Meeker opened the window, then went downstairs for a beer.

He crossed the dusty street, skirted a row of tied saddle horses, and went into the saloon. He stood at the bar with his beer and looked around. Five men were playing serious poker at one of the tables, and Meeker saw Howard Kearn there, too drunk to play and too stubborn to quit.

Meeker's acquaintance with Howard Kearn was slight; nevertheless he felt an interest in Kearn because of Tim Manlove. It was part of the way Meeker looked at the world. He owed Manlove more than he could ever repay, and he knew that Manlove and Marge Kearn had once planned to be married. Therefore, Meeker felt compelled to look kindly upon Marge's brother.

He pulled a chair away from a nearby table and straddled it to watch the game.

As calculated a chicken-picking as he had ever seen was going on. The man on Kearn's right was tipping the bottle, making sure Kearn stayed drunk enough. The other three were openly manipulating the cards, taking his money to be split later. Yet they were clever crooks, allowing Kearn to win a hand now and then, though never enough to make up for his losses.

For half an hour Meeker watched the play. Kearn handled his cards in a reckless, plunging

26

fashion. The man was a fool, Meeker thought, living from one burst of optimism to another. When he lost, he turned morose and sullen, and when he won the token pots, he shouted and slapped the table.

Meeker took out his tobacco sack and began to roll a cigarette. He was surprised when one of the men turned his head and said, 'Either get in the game or move away. You make me nervous.'

'That isn't what makes you nervous,' Meeker said. He nodded toward the space between the tables. 'Suppose I was sitting here playing solitaire? Would that make you nervous too?'

'Listen,' the man said, pointing at Meeker. 'I don't like the Army to start with, so don't give me any big mouth.' By accident or otherwise, his hand struck Meeker's, knocking the makings out of Meeker's fingers.

Meeker said, 'Now you've spilled my tobacco. Clumsy bastard, aren't you?' He watched the man's eyes, and moved a fraction of an instant before the other did.

A wild swing slid past Meeker's face. Meeker caught the extended arm, turned in the chair and yanked the man face down on the table. Still holding the arm, he whipped out of his chair and around the table and pulled violently.

The man's head and shoulders hit the sawdust with a thump. Meeker reached down

27

and took him by the nose so hard that blood spurted between the fingers of Meeker's gauntlet. He drew the other to his feet, then sledged him squarely in the mouth with his fist. Meeker had a hard hand to begin with, and it was tightly bunched in the leather gauntlet, making it as solid as a rock. When the man's head rapped the table, it sounded like someone slapping a horse on the rump.

The hardcase groped for his pistol belt. Meeker hit him again, hard enough to make him go limp. Then he took the .44 out of the holster and sent it skidding across the sawdust-covered floor.

Grasping the man's neckerchief and twisting it into a choke, Meeker hauled the other clear and flung him bodily through the swinging doors.

He turned back to the table and stopped. Howard Kearn was sitting up at the table, surprisingly sober, and the black maw of his handgun was holding the other three men motionless.

Kearn said, 'You almost got a hole in your back from one of these gents, Lieutenant.'

The whiskey put a glassy sheen to his eyes, but he had a steady hand when he reached for the money. 'The quickest way to find out who cheats at cards, gents, is to be a little too drunk. So since you've been cheating me for the last hour, I think the table stakes are mine.' He took off his hat, raked the money into it and clapped it quickly on his head without spilling a coin. He kicked his chair back and stood up. 'Ready to go, Lieutenant?'

'I'd say we've both worn out our welcomes,' Meeker said, stepping backward to the door. Howard Kearn joined him on the porch. He holstered his revolver and smiled.

'You did me a favor,' he said. 'I wanted out of that game, but the odds were too stacked. I figured I couldn't make it.' Kearn took Meeker's arm and guided him on down the street. 'Generally, I'm not too friendly with the Army. Maybe you heard about that.'

'I did, but I don't keep a head full of details or give a damn about listening to them.' Meeker looked up and down the street. 'It might be healthy for you and me to get out of sight. You can share my hotel room if you haven't any place to go.'

'Thanks,' Kearn said. He patted his hat. 'I must have six hundred dollars here. That's enough to get away from the old man and start out on my own. They tell me land in north Texas is so cheap it's almost given away.'

'That may be all it's worth,' Meeker said. He turned his head as a man's heavy footfall sounded on the walk.

The town marshal came up and peered at them. 'I guess you're the one, soldier. That was an inelegant way to treat one of our number one citizens.'

Meeker said, 'If he's a number one citizen,

29

spare me the culls. Do you want to arrest me, Marshal?'

'No,' the marshal said. 'But I wouldn't hang around town.' He glanced at Howard Kearn as though he had just recognized him. 'I know without asking that you had something to do with this.'

'An innocent bystander,' Howard said.

'I was told about you holding a gun on 'em.'

Meeker laughed. 'Did they mention the aces up their sleeves?' He touched Kearn's arm. 'Let's go get some sleep.'

They left the marshal standing on the walk and cut across to the hotel. The clerk was dozing when they passed through the lobby. The lamps had been turned down and Meeker and Kearn went up the stairs without disturbing the man. The hallway light was poor—Meeker had to bend down to find the keyhole. As he tried to insert the key he heard a sound at the far end of the darkened hall. Kearn heard it too and both men turned.

Their warning was slight, the metallic click of a rifle trigger against the sear. Both men dived for opposite walls as a rose petal of muzzle flame, shockingly bright, illuminated the far end of the hall for a split second. Splinters exploded from the door frame. Meeker clawed at the flap of his holster. The rifleman fired again and again, moving his gun slightly for each shot.

A bullet slammed into the wall near

Meeker's head. Howard Kearn shot twice and missed. Meeker came to a conclusion and placed a shot on either side of the last muzzle flash. He heard the clatter of the dropped rifle. Then there was a sliding, clawing sound as a sodden weight dropped to the floor.

Now people in the other rooms were stirring. In a moment the clerk came dashing up the stairs, followed by several other men, the marshal among them.

Kearn, lighting the wall lamps, was scratching matches on the wall, ignoring the clerk's distressed protests.

The marshal pushed his way down the hall to look at the dead man. 'Drilled dead center,' he said to Kearn. 'This looks like murder. Did you shoot him?'

'I shot twice,' Kearn said, 'but I missed him. Can't figure it out, because I put both slugs right over the muzzle flash.'

'I got him with my second shot,' Meeker said. 'He fired four times and missed by a good margin each time. Now no man lives long in this country unless he aims better than that, so I figured he was holding the rifle way out to one side, just in case someone like Kearn put a couple of bullets over the muzzle flash. So I shot first to one side, then the other.'

The marshal looked doubtful. 'You thought of all that while he was shootin'?'

'Can you tell me a better time to think fast?' Meeker asked.

'It don't sound right,' the marshal said. 'It's just your word against a dead man's that you didn't start the fight.' He looked at the man, who was staring vacantly at the ceiling. The marks of Meeker's fists were still fresh on his face; he had not lived long enough to grow a bruise.

'You admit he was drilled dead center,' Kearn said. 'You think he could have fired four shots after that?'

The marshal stroked his mustache. 'You've got a point there. All right, I guess that settles it. But it's a hell of a way for a fist fight to turn out.'

'He picked his own way to go,' Meeker said flatly.

'All right, folks.' The marshal began herding people away. 'Go on back to bed and let the law handle this. Come on now, that's fine. Clear the hall.'

Meeker unlocked his door and stepped inside. Kearn followed, closed and bolted the door, while Meeker lighted the lamp and extracted the two empties from his pistol.

Kearn said, 'Most of the time I drink because the old man hates it, but right now I could use one, because I need it.' He looked steadily at Paul Meeker. 'I'd like to own your nerve.'

'What nerve?' Meeker held out his hand so Kearn could see it tremble.

'Most men would try to hide a thing like

that,' Kearn said. 'My old man would. Maybe I would, too.'

'Why would you say that man out there had to die?' Meeker asked reflectively, ignoring Kearn's comment.

Kearn thought a minute, then said, 'I guess he couldn't take the licking in the saloon.'

Paul Meeker sat down and pulled off his boots. 'Not that. It's too simple, and man is indeed a more complicated animal. Have you ever wondered how many men have died in this world because the sight of another man brought to the surface hidden hates?'

'No, I've never thought about it.'

'For a short time,' Meeker said, 'I was a symbol to that man. A symbol of something evil. Maybe he guessed I was a better killer than he. Having to prove it leaves me with an uncomfortable feeling.'

Kearn laughed softly. 'I like you, Meeker, even if you are Army. If it's all right with you, I'll ride back with you in the morning.'

'Fair enough,' Meeker said and stretched out on the bed.

* * *

Tim Manlove ate breakfast, then went to the corral to gather his unshod Indian ponies and rope them together into a string abreast. Brady was already at the corral. Sam and Marge Kearn came from the house to watch, for

33

Manlove was good with a rope.

A thread of dust to the east marked an approaching rider.

Kearn said, 'Must be Howard.'

Howard Kearn came straight to the corral and dismounted. Seeing that the ponies were ready to go, he said, 'Give me five minutes to put some grub in a sack and I'll ride drag to Antlers Spring.'

The offer was too astounding for Manlove to say anything.

Sam Kearn gaped. 'What's at Antlers Spring that you'd want?'

'Lieutenant Meeker and I had a real whoop-up in Lordsburg. I rode most of the way with him. We're going to play some cards tonight.' He turned abruptly and walked toward the house.

'Now don't that beat all?' Sam asked. 'Sober, too. Who's Meeker?'

'A Yankee,' Manlove said. 'You wouldn't like him, Sam.'

Howard came from the house ten minutes later, carrying a heavy bedroll and two saddlebags.

The old man asked, 'You need all that to go to Antlers Spring?'

'Yep,' Howard cut out three horses. When he had them on a lead rope, he turned. 'I'm not coming back, Pa. So I'll say goodbye now.'

'What kind of damn nonsense is this?' the old man roared. 'You git in the house and stay there until I tell you to come out.'

'My mind's made up,' Howard said stiffly. 'Meeker was right. I'll never amount to anything around you, Pa.'

'You're drunk,' Kearn said and pushed him toward the house. 'Now you do what I say, by God, or—'

'Let me go, Pa.'

They struggled a moment, then Howard whipped up his gun and brought the barrel down across the crown of his father's hat.

Marge gasped as the old man fell. Howard looked down at him and spoke softly. 'You had that coming to you, Pa.'

He turned to his horse and stepped into the saddle. Manlove said, 'Brady, you and Howard go on. I'll come later.'

Getting Kearn to his shoulder was not easy but he managed it. He carried the old man into the house. Marge ran on ahead to open the doors. Manlove took Kearn to his room and put him down on the bed. There was a deep split in his scalp.

'I'll get some water and cloth,' Marge said. 'He'll have a headache over this.'

Manlove waited in the kitchen. Twenty minutes later she came back and put the pan down. 'Like I said, he has a real headache.' She brushed hair away from her face. 'You'd better go if you want to catch the others.'

'I wouldn't leave you here alone,' Manlove said. 'When your father's on his feet, I'll go back.'

'Pa wouldn't think it was right, you and me here alone.'

'Do you care about that?'

She shook her head. 'No, I want you to stay.'

'Then that ends the matter,' Manlove said gruffly.

*　　　*　　　*

The day's heat was turning the kitchen into a furnace. Outside, shimmers rose from the tawny dust. Marge went to the wooden sink and washed the breakfast dishes. Sweat ran down her cheeks and dripped from her chin.

She said, 'I'm always afraid this time of the year, when the hands are laid off and we're alone. I get so tired of always watching and listening.'

'Why doesn't Sam keep a couple of hands on all year?'

'We can't afford that. Sometimes I wonder why we stay on. Things never seem to get better. Diablito keeps us out of the mountains where there's springs and some pasture.' She put her hands on the edge of the sink and stood that way for a moment. 'I guess the Lord meant for people's lives to be hard.'

Manlove had no argument for her—he had often felt the same way.

With Kearn temporarily unable to work, the day's chores fell to Manlove. At nightfall he went to the corral to cut out and saddle a horse. When he returned, Sam Kearn was in the kitchen drinking coffee. The old man's head was bandaged. He looked up sullenly.

Manlove said, 'That seep about a mile north of here was getting muddy so I cleaned it out.' He pegged his rifle and washed his hands and face at the sink.

'I'm in your debt,' Kearn growled.

'To hell with your debt,' Tim Manlove said bluntly.

'What got into that boy?' Kearn asked. 'Can you tell me that?'

'You rode him too hard once too often.' Manlove looked steadily at Kearn. 'Can you manage now? I'll have to explain this delay to the captain and that won't be the easiest thing to do.'

'I can manage,' Kearn said. 'Are you going to make a night ride?'

'A man alone is safer at night,' Manlove said. 'And, Sam, I'll look after Howard all I can while he's at the station.'

Relief softened Kearn's severe expression. He nodded, got up and walked unsteadily into another part of the house.

Marge Kearn looked at Manlove. 'You haven't said when I'll see you again, Tim.'

'I don't know when,' he told her. She came up to him and into his arms without a word. He kissed her gently, yet there was a fire in him that she could feel. When they parted, he said,

37

'We shouldn't make plans now, Marge.'

'We have to,' she said. 'I've lived from day to day for a year. I can't go on like that.'

'I won't say goodbye now. You understand, Marge?'

'Promise you'll come for me.'

'I wish I could,' he said and went outside to saddle his horse.

When he was some distance from the place, he turned and looked back at the light coming from the slits in the adobe walls—faint smears of yellow brightness that faded as he rode away.

Not for a moment did he forget that he was alone and vulnerable to attack. Manlove knew the Apaches well and, pound for pound, he considered them the most savage fighting machine on the face of the earth. They were a people born in legend, surrounded by it, steeped in it, and their great weapon was fear. Never great in numbers, they had learned to attack with deadly precision and suddenness out of nowhere and fade away as fast. He knew their tricks, their habits—even their thoughts—and somehow the knowing had destroyed his fear. Even now, riding alone, he felt as much the hunter as the hunted.

He kept close attention upon the surrounding land. Even in the moonlight he could follow the trail Brady and Howard Kearn had left—they had been moving fast, for so many horses would be a temptation to the

Apaches.

The fact that he found no Indian sign only increased his alertness. Apaches would do just about anything except needlessly risk their lives. Not that they were cowards—they did not even have a word for fear in their language. But their purpose was to kill and harass, not die—a goal a good soldier could understand. Some years back, while serving in the Sioux country, Manlove had been amazed at the heedless way the plains Indians would attack, fanatics to the last man, careless of danger. But not the Apaches.

Too, the Sioux rarely raided more than fifty miles from their camps, while the Apaches roamed like the wind. A band of five would raid, then pop up the next day sixty miles away and raid again, only to charge a hundred miles into Mexico and loot there.

Every step Manlove tracked Brady's cavvy intensified his hunter's instincts. Brady was moving fast and stood a good chance of getting through. That would leave the Apaches angry, looking for someone to kill and Manlove approached each potential ambush along the trail with an eye to turning it to his own advantage.

His thinking was, he recognized with a wry smile, pure Apache—he, too, wanted to kill. Drifting silently through the moonlight, choosing spots on the trail where his horse's hoofs made the least sound, he sat his saddle

39

loosely, giving no sign of being even fully awake. He knew the twisted Apache pride—they seldom shot an outwardly unsuspecting man out of the saddle without an instant's warning. The warning might come too late, perhaps simultaneously with the twang of a bow or the crack of a rifle—but always in time for the victim's last instant of consciousness to register the nature of his killer.

The attack, when it came, came with the suddenness of heat lightning. With the first sound of the inhuman screech, Manlove dropped behind his horse, gripping the animal with his thighs. As a shadow leaped up from the ground he fired under the horse's neck, like a Sioux. Two rifles crashed almost simultaneously. Manlove's bullet caught the Apache in the breastbone, knocking him flat.

Manlove wheeled the horse around as another Apache fired from the opposite side. He felt the bullet burn along the top of his boot and thumbed two fast shots in return. The second Indian lurched to his feet, collapsed, and Manlove saw a third for an instant, then lost him in the darkness. The Apache had flattened himself against the earth.

To smoke him out, Manlove began to ride in a circle, gradually closing it in. Three times around—four—and a black shape sprang up, muzzle flame flashed.

Manlove felt his horse falter. He kicked free as the animal went down, then rolled to a sitting position. He fired on his knees, the long barrel of the pistol resting across his forearm.

Stumbling from the shock of the bullet, the Apache flung his arms wide and fell. After a long silence Manlove rose slowly to his feet. He made sure the Apaches were dead, then gathered their weapons and ammunition.

A long walk lay ahead of him, but Manlove did not mind. He got his canteen and blankets, tied the captured rifles and ammunition together into a shoulder pack, and struck off.

There would be cursing in Diablito's camp in the morning. The three braves were the first losses Diablito had suffered out of pitched battle in a year, except for the one Sam Kearn had killed, and the wily old ghost would be hungry for revenge.

* * *

Manlove arrived at Antlers Spring Station shortly before dawn and, being afoot, was nearly shot for an Apache. When he was passed onto the station, he sat down before the CO's quarters and waited for the guard to get Captain Dane out of his bunk.

Dane came out, pulling up his suspenders. 'Are you practicing for the Infantry?' he asked. He picked up the bundle of rifles and turned. 'Come in. I'll pour you a drink.'

Manlove pushed himself erect wearily. In Dane's office, he sat down and accepted a drink. He told Dane about the gunfight in the desert.

'Of course they were after the horses,' Dane said. 'You made a good buy from Kearn. They're Navaho ponies, aren't they?'

'Howard got them some place up north,' Manlove said, with purposeful vagueness. 'Captain, I brought those Apache rifles back for a couple of reasons. If you'll take a look at them, sir, you may notice the same thing I did.'

Dane turned up the lamp and examined the rifles carefully. He frowned and said, 'Sixty-six model Winchesters. They look pretty average to me.'

'Well, it struck me right off that if I was stealing guns and ammunition, the chances of my picking up all the same model and caliber would be mighty slim.'

Dane swore and slapped the desk. 'Of course! All forty-four rimfire. These were likely sold to Diablito.'

'That's what I think,' Manlove said. As he spoke, a man crossed the porch and came toward Dane's office. Howard Kearn stopped in the doorway, and Dane motioned him in.

'I was sleeping on the guardhouse roof and the noise woke me,' Howard said. He looked at the rifles on Dane's desk. 'Apache?' He glanced at Dane for permission, then picked one up and turned it over in his hands, frowning. 'Funny, you don't see many of these forty-four rimfires any more. But just a couple of months

42

ago I saw a fella with a whole case of these.'

'Suppose you tell us about that,' Dane said softly. 'Take a chair, Kearn.'

Howard sat down and rolled a cigarette. 'I was in Navaho country after ponies,' he said. 'Now and then I buy some stock from this fella.'

'Put a name to him,' Manlove said.

Kearn hesitated. 'Joe Berry. He's in the horse business.'

Dane swore softly. 'I know that man. When I was on my first assignment, he cheated two of my men at cards, then shot and seriously wounded one. I personally ran him out of Prescott with a bullet in his arm. Four years later we had a disagreement over the ownership of some horses. A year after that, he bankrolled a cathouse down near the border and put half my company down with disease. Berry and I came to blows and I closed his place and advised him to clear out of Arizona Territory.'

'He didn't take you seriously, sir,' Manlove said, drawing a scowl from Dane. 'Since Diablito only raids for women and money, he's probably buying rifles and ammunition from Berry.'

Dane said, 'Every tenet of military strategy teaches that you must cut off the enemy's lines of supply before you can defeat him in the field. Through the years, we've run ourselves ragged chasing Diablito, but he's never grown

43

weaker.' He paused to think. 'I could ask the U.S. Marshal—no, there isn't enough to go on. We may have to take care of this ourselves.'

'We can't spare the time and the men,' Manlove said.

'Sometimes the long way around is the quickest.' He bit off the end of a cigar. 'This is the only break we've had in a year. We can't afford to let it go by.' He looked at Kearn. 'You say Berry's in the horse-trading business?'

'Yes.'

'You and Sergeant Manlove could approach him, then—ostensibly to trade.'

'Hell with that kind of duty,' Howard said gruffly. 'I'm no Judas.' But he seemed uncertain. 'Besides, I'm heading for Texas.'

'There's more than one way of getting away from your old man,' Manlove said. 'You'd be on your own this trip and doing something for someone else besides.'

'I could give you scout's pay,' Dane said. 'Three dollars a day and a dollar for your horse. Kearn, you left the Army with a stink following you. You do a job like this, and it'll take that stink away.'

'Who gives a damn about the Army?' Howard demanded.

'You give a damn,' said Manlove. 'Captain, I'd like to have Lieutenant Meeker go along. The two of us will find Berry's camp.'

'Oh, hell,' Kearn said. 'I'll go with you, but

we'll have to go as civilians. If Berry thought you were Army, he'd open fire and I couldn't stop it.'

'Why? Has he stolen some Army mounts?' Dane asked.

Kearn grinned. 'Captain, Berry's stolen everything at least once.'

Dane said, 'Suppose I continue the routine patrols for thirty days, making shallow penetrations into the hills in order to show Diablito we're still active, yet not deep enough to draw his fire. That should give you time enough to find Berry's Navaho contact and meeting place with Diablito or his men. You could pass for a top horse wrangler, Manlove. Meeker doesn't have the experience, but I don't think that will arouse too much suspicion. Most horse hunters break in new men, or take a greenhorn along for the flunky work.' He looked at Howard Kearn. 'Does that sound all right with you?'

'We want to be buyers, not hunters,' Kearn said. 'Berry claims that country as his own. He lets me in because I'm a buyer.'

'How did you meet him?' Dane asked.

'A card game. And we got drunk together.'

'I guess that's recommendation enough for some people,' Manlove said, rising from the chair. 'When do we leave, Captain?'

'Late in the evening. Get some sleep now. Meeker will handle the details.'

Manlove and Howard Kearn left the office,

but stopped on the porch. The sky was growing light, a pale gray with a hint of pink along the horizon. Kearn rolled another cigarette, then passed his makings to Manlove. He said, 'If anyone had told me I'd spend a month on the trail with you, I'd have said he was crazy.' He laughed softly. 'I'm a fool. I ought to be riding south tomorrow like I planned.' He glanced briefly at Manlove. 'Is the old man all right?'

'You hit him pretty hard.'

'Wish I hadn't. He's all right, though?'

'He's got a lump on his head and he'll have a scar, but he's all right. Are you?'

'What do you mean?'

'You feel any better after hitting him?'

'Yeah, but it didn't last long.' Kearn stamped on his cigarette. 'Tim, is there anything to this business about blood being thicker than water?'

'I don't know,' Manlove said. 'I've got brothers and sisters somewhere, but I don't feel anything for them. Howard, in some ways we're alike. Your old man kept pushing you away because he didn't know how to get close to you. Mine pushed me out because there was nothing else he could do. Neither of us has ever forgiven them for it.'

'I guess that's right,' Howard said. 'It sure as hell sounds right.'

46

CHAPTER FOUR

Manlove took a bath, went to bed and slept out the day. The intense heat made sleeping uncomfortable and he awoke when Lieutenant Paul Meeker came into the quarters. Army habit brought Manlove halfway to his feet, but Meeker pushed him back.

'There's no time for that.'

Meeker wore an old pair of blue denim pants and a checkered shirt under a light canvas coat. Around his waist he wore a cartridge belt with a most unmilitary slant to it, and at the bottom of the arc was holstered a bone-handled .44.

'You look like Jesse James, Lieutenant,' Manlove said.

Meeker laughed and tossed a bundle of clothes on the bed. Manlove put them on. He found a pistol wrapped in the shirt. The holster was Mexican, open-topped, the garden variety for civilians who sometimes needed a weapon in a hurry.

They walked to headquarters and into Dane's office. Howard Kearn was already there, talking with Dane. Meeker and Manlove sat down.

'Here's a hundred and seventy dollars in gold,' Dane said, handing the pouch to Paul Meeker. 'The horses you're riding are all stock too old for duty. Trade at the first opportunity,

47

because an Army mount can be spotted a mile away on a cloudy day. Likely you're going to need a pack horse and some supplies. Is there anything you'd like to ask?'

'Couldn't we use those new Winchesters?' Meeker asked.

'I think you'll be better off carrying these three forty-fours,' Dane said. 'Don't you agree, Kearn?'

'They're light on power, but I think it's a good notion.'

There was little more to discuss. Dane shook hands all around and went outside with them. The horses were brought up. The three men mounted and headed out, taking the Lordsburg road. Manlove planned to swing north before reaching the town, and pick up the Fort Defiance trail later.

The night turned cool. They stopped late in the evening, ate cold meat and biscuits and rested the horses. While they ate, Howard spoke of their destination, a small mining town four days' ride to the north.

'We can buy horses in Reserve,' he said. 'I know my way around the town.'

'How far is it to Fort Defiance?' Meeker asked.

'From here, a week. But I don't think we ought to stop there. We can angle northwest from Reserve. Pretty wild country for traveling, but it's a trail I've used before. The Injuns have some superstition about it, so you

48

can have a fire at night, and a hot meal.' He paused to think. 'We ought to be in the monument country in ten days. There ain't nothing there but wild horses, Mormons and Piutes.'

'And Joe Berry,' Meeker said.

There was no better way really to know a man, Manlove was convinced, than to be with him ten days on the trail, especially in wild country where the rattlesnakes ran in pairs for safety. He decided that he did not know Howard Kearn at all—had never known him. Kearn was a good man on the trail, a willing worker, a silent man who did not rub your nerves raw with talking unless he had something to say.

Manlove had thought Kearn a belligerent young man with a grudge against authority, a man who drank unpredictably and too heavily. Now the sergeant was inclined to the opinion that this behavior was a defense rather than a true indication of character. Paul Meeker had a bottle with him and now and then took a drink of it. When he first produced it, Manlove expected Kearn to lower its contents considerably, but the youth took a swig and thereafter let it alone. It was then that Manlove decided that Kearn did not really like booze at all, but drank because his father hated drinking. Thinking about it during their long days of travel, Manlove began to understand how old man Kearn's strength, his unerring

49

judgment and annoying habit of always being right could build in the boy a desire to do everything wrong just to prove his individuality.

The land changed as they moved north. They passed through hellish mountain passes, where the air was bitter cold at night and the bottom lay a thousand feet below—yawning canyons and streams looking like pieces of bright, bent metal. They passed through desert country—hills of sand constantly altered by winds—and for a time they rested in timbered stretches where the water was good and a night fire made life almost comfortable.

They could see the monument country long before they reached it, and one look was enough to show Manlove why men called it that. Jutting tall from the desert were flat-topped buttes, wind-worn, left standing after all the earth around them had eroded away.

'That's real wild-horse country,' said Manlove.

'Not far to go now,' Howard Kearn said. 'Three days.'

'Any idea where Berry's camp will be?'

'This time of year he works westward. I know the water holes and good camps.' Kearn fell silent, nudged his horse into motion.

The next day they were on the desert floor, moving westerly. Manlove saw Indian and wild-horse signs and, in the distance, smoke from a fireplace. People lived here, but he could not imagine why.

Joe Berry's camp was near a spring at the base of a box canyon, a huge fissure in the side of a towering butte. Berry's greeting was not friendly. He had four men with him, a wagon and a dozen pack horses. The men stood rifles at ready as Kearn went forward; Manlove and Paul Meeker stayed back, close enough to hear, yet far enough away to indicate that they would not advance without a welcome.

'I was hoping you'd have some more ponies,' Kearn said, swinging down.

'Haven't been into the Navaho country for a spell,' Berry said. He glanced coldly at Manlove and Meeker. 'Generally, I don't like company.'

'Partners,' Kearn said. 'We threw in together since I last saw you. I didn't think you'd mind.'

Joe Berry scowled. He was a wiry man, tall and hipless. His face was hairy and he struck Manlove as the kind who only took a bath when he had a river to ford. Berry made a slight motion to one of his men and the man came forward. He walked around Meeker and Manlove, studied the pack horse. When he reached up to untie a knot, Manlove shook his head.

'Don't fool with that, friend.'

'Why not?' the man asked.

'Because I say.'

Joe Berry said, 'Go ahead and look, Jeff.' He

51

smiled. 'If he's got nothin' to hide, he won't mind.'

'Ask me first,' Tim Manlove said.

'I don't ask a man for anything in my camp,' Berry said flatly. 'Ain't that right, Kearn?'

'Hell, let him have his look,' Kearn said.

That seemed to settle it in Jeff's mind. He began to untie the knot. Manlove turned without haste and hit him across the forearm with his rifle barrel. Cursing, clutching his arm, Jeff stepped back.

'You're right unfriendly,' Berry said.

'Not unfriendly. I'm not nosy either. I don't prowl your things, and you don't prowl mine.'

For a moment Berry said nothing, then he shrugged. 'Get down and have some beans.'

'That sounds fine,' Manlove said. As he stamped his legs he looked at Jeff. 'If you want to look, go ahead.'

Jeff scratched his head and asked, 'How does a man figure you, anyway?'

'You don't.' Manlove picked up a tin plate. While he served himself, Howard Kearn introduced him to Berry. Manlove only nodded, and did not offer to shake hands.

'I've got a buyer for about thirty Injun ponies,' Howard said. 'I needed some help, so I brought them along.' He nodded at Manlove and Meeker.

'I haven't got thirty ponies,' Berry said. 'What'll you pay?'

'The usual—ten dollars a head.'

52

Berry scratched his beard. 'I wouldn't want to do business with a man who was too fussy about his stock.'

'We're not,' Manlove said. 'This is a Texas buyer.' What Berry meant was plain enough. The horses would be stolen, and probably not only from the Indians. Berry wanted them to end up a long way from here.

'All right,' he said finally. 'I got word last week that some Indians had ponies to trade. Some branded stock there. Is that all right?'

'Fine,' said Kearn. 'Where can we spread our blankets?'

Berry indicated a spot some distance from his camp. Manlove and Paul Meeker laid their blankets out close together. Meeker asked, 'Would he be fool enough to steal branded stock?'

'No,' Manlove answered. 'They're from Apache raids.'

'Think Berry will make a contact?'

'Maybe. He likes money and he thinks Kearn is a damned fool. Hey, Howard, come here.' He waited until Kearn joined them. 'What's your idea about this? If Berry makes a contact, we can't let him go through with it.'

Howard said, 'We may not have much choice. I don't know—I've never been with him when he made a contact. Watch out, here comes Jeff.'

Berry's partner lumbered over. 'Berry says we'll break camp at dawn.'

53

'Hell, we just got here,' Manlove protested.

Jeff grinned. 'You want horses, we'll leave at dawn. Joe don't want to try and handle a herd that size, not with just three of us.' He turned and went back.

'Let's bed down,' Manlove said. 'Dawn comes quick enough, and this is no place to be asleep. Kearn, you stay awake for a few hours. Call me and I'll spell you.'

'We don't have to do that,' Howard said.

Paul Meeker grinned. 'Don't you get the idea? When Berry sees one of us awake all night, he'll have to keep someone awake to see what we're up to.' He slapped Howard on the shoulder. 'Go on, take the first trick.'

Manlove stretched out and folded his hands behind his head. Long shadows were forming. Berry's fire grew brighter as the darkness deepened.

'I wonder where he keeps his horses,' Meeker said softly.

'Probably in some box canyon,' Manlove said. 'These buttes are full of short draws. We don't care where he keeps his horses. I'd just like to know if he goes into Apache country, or do the Navahos.'

'It's something to worry about,' Meeker admitted. 'If he only deals in the Navahos, we're in a blind alley. We couldn't break away from Berry without making him suspicious, and if we fought it out with him, the Navahos would never lead us to Diablito's men.'

54

'We could keep pushing him, like we're in a hurry. If he has a middleman, he might go around him this time,' Manlove said.

'Like finding a button in a dark barracks,' Meeker said and closed his eyes.

Manlove slept, and Howard woke him three hours later. Taking his rifle along, Manlove stirred up their fire and looked over at Berry's camp. Joe Berry was up. At length he motioned Manlove over.

Berry had coffee cooking and offered some. 'Noticed your rifle right away,' he said. 'You don't see many forty-four rimfires any more.'

'Got it off a dead Apache,' Manlove said. 'I like it. Light, good balance. Not much for game, but for man shooting it'll do.'

Berry studied him. 'You do much man shooting?'

'Some,' Manlove admitted.

'This other fella you got with you, he don't say much.'

'Too young to know anything,' Manlove said. 'You make rotten coffee.'

'Don't drink it, then. Yeah, I thought he looked pretty young.'

Manlove shrugged. 'Sometimes it's easier to get rid of a kid than a grown man. I'm not like you, Berry. I don't have two men I can trust.'

'I thought you worked for Kearn.'

Manlove laughed. 'Mister, they work for me, only they don't know it.' He helped himself to more coffee.

'Thought you didn't like the java.'

'I said it was rotten, not that I didn't like it.'

Berry grinned. 'You mean just what you say, don't you?'

'All the time.'

'Kearn a friend of yours?'

'Don't insult me,' Manlove said. 'If something good comes along, I'll leave him for the buzzards to pick. Quickest way I know of dissolving a partnership.' He studied Berry. 'You ever try it?'

'Never had to, yet.' Berry crossed his legs and leaned forward. 'When this horse deal is through, maybe we could talk. I've been thinking about expanding a little. Put on another man maybe. You got any religion?'

'What's that?' Manlove asked.

Joe Berry laughed softly. 'That's what I thought. You know, a man can make a fortune off these Mormons. Cheat 'em blind and they don't even hold it against you. Ain't it hell to be so trusting?'

'I don't trust anybody,' Manlove said flatly. 'And I wouldn't hire on to you.'

'Why not? I pay good.'

'I don't hire out. Partners, yes, but no hire.' He swished the coffee around in the cup, drank it and threw the grounds into the fire. 'Jeff and the other man your partners?'

Berry shook his head. 'I pay 'em wages. They're both stupid.'

'I'm not,' Manlove said. 'Fifty-fifty after

expenses.'

Berry was silent a moment, then said, 'You'll have to take care of 'em. Pick your own time.'

'After we get the horses. I'll need help until then. Once we get the stock on lead ropes, I'll drop back and lose both of them. You tell your men to stay out of it.'

'All right. You don't have much of a feeling for anything, do you?'

'Am I supposed to?'

'No,' Berry said. 'It don't pay. I found that out when I was a kid. Me and six others ate out of one dish. If you didn't use your elbows and fists, you went hungry. I always got mine, and I always aim to.'

Manlove stood up and walked back to his own camp. He squatted by the fire and waited until Berry turned in. He heard Paul Meeker stir slightly.

'Make your pact with the devil, Sergeant?'

Manlove spoke without turning his head. 'I told him I'd throw in with him, and after we got the horses and he got paid, I'd drop back, kill both of you and join him. When I drop behind, that'll be the signal for you and Howard to cut down on Berry's two friends. I told him I wanted them to stay clear, that I'd handle it myself.'

'Sounds touchy,' Meeker said.

'Yes. We can't afford any mistakes. I'll take Joe Berry. You take Jeff, and Howard the other one. Meanwhile get some sleep.'

Sitting in the dark, Tim Manlove had time to think. The fact that Berry could lay his hands on branded stock proved that he was dealing with the Apaches, who no doubt wanted to trade for the things Diablito's campaign needed. Diablito would not want whiskey or blankets—he had need of cartridges and rifles. Somewhere, probably not far away, Berry had his cache. Manlove wished he knew where it was; and the more he thought about it, the more specific his ideas grew. He waited until his fire had died down.

Finally he shook Howard Kearn awake, and cautioned him with a gesture to be quiet.

Manlove breathed his question: 'Berry must have a supply wagon—where does he keep it?'

'Around the other side of the butte, I think. I've seen him send Jeff for something—coffee, flour—he's never gone more than an hour.'

'I don't guess they'll miss us for an hour,' Manlove said. 'Lieutenant, you still awake?'

'I heard you,' Meeker said. 'Don't be stupid, now, Sergeant.'

'Just want to take a look, sir. Come on, Kearn.'

'What do you think you're going to do?' Meeker asked. 'Suppose Berry comes over?'

'Then you'll have to fight it out with him,' Manlove said. 'He won't believe we're taking a constitutional.' He moved over and bunched his blankets up so that they resembled a man sleeping. 'If Berry's got a jug hidden out, do

58

you want me to bring you back a swig, Lieutenant?'

'You go to the devil. And come back safe.'

Manlove and Kearn left the camp silently on their hands and knees. When they were forty yards away, they stood up.

Kearn asked, 'What the hell are we really doing this for, I'd like to know?'

'Don't you have any curiosity at all?'

'Not when I can get killed for it.' Kearn sighed. 'Well, let's go. If I turned back now, I'd always wonder whether I had good sense or no guts.'

CHAPTER FIVE

Leaving the short canyon where Berry had his camp, Manlove and Kearn paused in the jumble of fallen rock by the edge of the butte.

'Which way?' Manlove asked. The night was dark and he could see only a short distance. Beyond lay the pale shadow of the desert floor and the outlines of distant buttes. 'It's got to be around here. It must be four miles to the nearest butte.'

'Let's try this way.' Kearn veered off to the right. 'I know some of this ground and I'm figuring on the time element.'

They worked their way carefully through the boulders, and finally came upon a bottleneck opening. Inside they found what they were looking for—Berry's wagon and a mess of crated and baled gear. There were coils of rope for fencing; posts; tools; rolls of wire—and crates of rifles. One contained three .44 rimfires, the other held an even dozen.

'There's his trading stock,' Kearn said softly. 'So what do we do? Wreck 'em? I can just see some buck killing my sister with one of these.'

'If we put a mark on them, we've tipped our hand to Berry,' said Manlove. He paused to think. 'All new. Still got grease on them. You know, it would be a real dirty trick to play on Berry, but if we could disable these rifles, Diablito's Apaches would get so mad they'd kill the bastard.'

'I've had one apart,' Howard said. 'Let's take out the firing pins.'

'No, the Apaches would make new ones out of nails. Look around and see if you can find a rifle rod. They used to pack a couple in each crate.' Kearn rummaged for the rod; Manlove took some .44 rimfire shells from his pocket and counted them out.

'Here's a rod,' Howard said. 'What are you going to do with the bullets?'

'Pull the lead and ram one halfway down each barrel.'

'Hell, use Berry's ammunition. We may not be able to spare it.'

'No, he'd see a busted box and want to know

60

why. Fifteen rounds won't leave me that short.' Manlove pressed the lead nose of bullets against the boxes, expanded the brass cases and handed the slugs to Howard. 'These brass receivers are none too strong, anyway. When they fire the first round, either the barrels will bulge or the receivers will split.'

'You've got a sly, mean mind,' Kearn said.

One by one, they plugged the barrels. The job took thirty minutes; then they went back to their camp.

Paul Meeker was awake. 'For God's sake, where have you been?'

'Baying at the moon,' Kearn said. 'Go to sleep.'

'But—'

'Good night, sir,' Manlove said and Meeker gave up in disgust.

Joe Berry was stirring at dawn. His fire burned high. Jeff left the camp while the third man, the one they called Pete, cooked breakfast. Berry waved for Manlove and the others to join him. By the time they were through eating, Jeff came back with a pack horse. He hunkered down and gulped his sidemeat and coffee while Berry saw that their horses were saddled.

'Got a five-day ride,' he said. 'I expect you have enough grub.'

'We'll manage,' Meeker said. 'Where are we going?'

'You'll find that out when you get there,'

Berry told him. He winked at Tim Manlove and emptied the coffee pot. 'You ever do any trading with Injuns?'

'Nothing honest,' Manlove said.

Berry laughed. 'Talk Apache?'

'No,' Manlove said. 'Do you, Kearn?'

'A few words,' Howard Kearn said. 'We doing business with the Apaches?'

'Would that bother you?'

'Guess not. But I wouldn't trust one farther'n I could see him.'

Jeff finished eating and they mounted, leaving everything scattered about just as they had finished with it. Pete led the way across the desert floor as the sun rose bright and hot. Berry and Manlove rode together, with Jeff behind them; Kearn and Meeker brought up the rear.

They wore out the day in silence. Because of his conversation with Berry, Manlove avoided Kearn and Meeker, even during the brief stops.

That night they camped in the rocks near a seep, and built no fire. Manlove lay in his blankets, smoked, and thought about these men and himself. If Berry's men and Kearn had really been buying horses this way he felt sorry, for it was a stupid, bitter, wasteful way to make a living. What good did it do Joe Berry? He would go to town four or five times a year, drink, gamble it away, or give it to some woman who would not remember his name. And men died because Joe Berry had to have his cheap pleasure.

It was a good feeling to be Army—Manlove felt his profession to be a coat of armor shielding him from decay. He had not felt this smug, this superior to anyone in a long time, and although he tried, he could not feel properly ashamed of his attitude. When this chore was over, he would bathe and dress in clean blues and come back to his civilized manners, and because he had this to look to he felt able to face whatever had to be done.

The next day took them into the mountains, and one day more brought them to an old burned-out ranch Manlove vaguely remembered. He could orient himself now and sensed the odds shifting a little in his favor.

Berry ordered camp made and a fire built and said nothing about Indians. Manlove did not ask; he knew the Apaches would see the smoke and come in. This area was obviously used as a meeting place.

Manlove scouted around the ruins of the ranch before it grew too dark to see. The place had been built partly of stone and two walls of a barn remained, but the roof, burned out, was nothing but charred beams.

A short ravine behind the barn drew his interest. At the far end he saw the white gleam of bone. He climbed down and took a closer look.

Three skeletons lay among the brush and rocks. From the size of the bones, Manlove

63

guessed he was looking at what remained of three young girls.

He made his way back, and told Meeker and Kearn what he had found.

Meeker asked, 'Do you suppose Berry knows about this?'

'I'd hate to bet he doesn't,' Kearn said. 'Let's take him now.'

'No,' Manlove said. 'Dane sent us to do a job, and we'll do it. This is all part of getting Diablito. Remember that.'

'But why would they kill those girls?' Kearn asked.

'Because they couldn't give Diablito a son,' Manlove said grimly. 'Let's act natural now, but stay awake.'

The Apache came before dark, a bandy-legged man in a stinking pair of cotton pants, carrying a rifle and a belt of shells over his shoulder.

He spoke to Berry only. 'You have guns? We have horses.'

'I need many horses,' Joe Berry said.

'We have many horses. Need many guns.'

Berry and the Indian sat down to parley at length. Finally the deal was made and the Apache left, promising to return with the horses. Berry had Jeff break open the pack on the spare horse and display the rifles and ammunition.

When the Apache came back he had three men with him and three strings of horses. Berry started talking again.

The horses were restless and moved about, and Howard saw a branded flank. He yelled in fury. Manlove saw the brand too—Sam Kearn's—and knew what it meant, but he was too late to stop Howard.

*   *   *

Kearn shot Joe Berry in the throat. Berry went down, bleeding, strangling, dying.

This was not the time, but there was no turning back now. Manlove fired, dropping the nearest Apache, then levered for a shot at Jeff, who had his pistol out and was fanning it.

Meeker gasped and went down, blood welling from his side, but he fired from the ground, twice, and hit Jeff in the chest with both shots.

The Apaches were running, but none escaped. Howard Kearn brought one down, then another. A bullet snapping the brim of Manlove's hat brought him around to face Pete. Holding the butt of his rifle against his hip, Manlove sprayed eight rounds as fast as he could work the lever and the man went down. Manlove did not know how many times he had hit him and did not care.

With the firing ended the silence was like a roar in his ears. Howard Kearn sat on the ground like a man belly-kicked and tears ran down his cheeks. The horses told their own story—the Kearn place had been raided, burned to the ground.

Manlove walked over and kneed Howard in the side. 'Come on, get up. Meeker's been hit, and we've got to get out of here.'

Kearn did not respond for a moment. At last he took hold of himself and went to Paul Meeker while Manlove caught up the frightened horses.

Manlove stripped the saddles from their own animals and saddled up three fresh ponies.

'That shooting is going to bring more Apaches,' he said. 'We've got to get the hell out of here, fast.'

He looked at Paul Meeker's gray face, and wondered just how far they would get.

They worked over Meeker, making a compress for his wound, bandaging him so tightly around the waist that he could not suppress a groan. Then they boosted him onto the horse in one swift motion, and he clung there as though hanging on were his dying wish.

Manlove led them out of the valley. He kept looking back at Meeker, but there was no need. Kearn rode beside Meeker, his grip on Meeker's arm holding the lieutenant in the saddle.

Any doubt Tim Manlove had had about Howard Kearn was gone—the boy would do to soldier with. Meeker fainted three times during the first hour, but Kearn would not let him fall. Finally Manlove pulled his horse aside and said, 'I'll take him for a while. Your arm must be ready to drop off.'

'No,' Kearn said flatly. 'I'll take care of him. He's the first man who ever looked at me like I was more than dung. Keep going. I'll make it.'

'Son, you've already made it,' Manlove said and rode on.

There was a moon, making night travel possible. By dark of the morning Manlove thought they could afford a short rest. He dismounted and went to help Kearn with Meeker, but the lieutenant shook his head.

'If I got—down, I'd never—get on again.'

'We've got to stop,' Kearn said. 'He'll die if we don't.'

'The Apaches will be ringing us come light,' Manlove said.

'Well, let 'em,' Kearn snapped. 'We can take care of Paul and dig in.' He took Manlove by the arm. 'Hell, you've always bragged how you'd like to lock horns with Diablito. Here's your chance.'

'Lieutenant, what do you think?' Manlove asked.

'Your—parade, Sergeant.'

'All right, let's get him off,' Manlove said. 'There's enough stub timber around here for a fire. We'll dig a trench like the damned Infantry do.'

They got Meeker down, removed the bullet and cauterized the wound. Kearn stripped to the waist in the biting mountain air, and worked until sweat rolled down his back.

Their fort was ten feet by ten, deep enough to stand in and shoot over the top. The piled dirt made a good breastwork, and Manlove built the fire in the pit, to hide its brightness. The heat was well contained. In the early hours of the morning, Paul Meeker slept, although he had a slight fever.

'Two against how many?' Kearn asked.

'I don't give a damn, do you?' Manlove stared over the breastwork. 'We've both lost more than we can afford. I'd as soon die here as somewhere else.'

Kearn nodded. 'You and Marge got a bad deal from me. I'm sorry about it now. Sorry about a lot of things.'

Manlove took out his tobacco and made a smoke, gave the sack and papers to Kearn. 'You still think your old man's better than you are?'

'No,' Howard said. 'I wish I could tell him so. I'd like to tell him that I don't have to booze it up and gamble and steal horses to get his attention. But it's too late. He's probably dead. Marge, too.'

'Yes, I figured that.' Manlove drew deep on his smoke and found it bitter, but briefly it masked his thoughts. 'Guess it won't matter so much, if I can take Diablito with me when I die.'

'Know him by sight?'

'I've never known a man, white or Apache, who's ever seen him. They say he's a ghost, that you can't see him. But that's Apache medicine talk on the reservation.'

Howard took a final pull on his smoke, then stubbed it out. 'Sorry about Meeker. We had some trouble together in Lordsburg. Side by side, all the way, like I always wanted it with Pa, if he'd of let me. You know what I mean?'

'Sure. Get some sleep.'

'No—I'll keep watch. If things turn out bad for me at dawn, I won't miss the sleep. And if we lick 'em, I'll have time for it.' He leaned back against the dirt wall. 'I ain't too scared, you know that?'

'You're all right,' Manlove said.

CHAPTER SIX

Dawn was gray and chilly with a raw wind raising dust and husking it along, moving the mountain grain by grain. Manlove and Kearn were waiting, rifles ready, pistols lying at hand, spare ammunition in a neat row so there would be no fatal fumbling.

They could see the terrain clearly, jumbled rock, scattered brush, and some stunted trees dying or dead. There was no sign of life, no movement. But the Apaches were out there, thirsting for revenge for their fallen brothers.

Experts at betrayal, they were doubly incensed by it when betrayed. Masters of ambush, they considered it a mortal sin to be the victims of ambush.

The first Apache popped up suddenly, screaming, shooting. Manlove and Kearn returned his fire too hastily, both missing. Manlove supposed this bit of poor marksmanship was an omen to them, a sign of invincibility, for they all began firing, showing glimpses of tawny skin in the hope of drawing out their enemy. Manlove counted at least seven Indians. He and Kearn merely pulled their heads down and let the bullets thud into the earth. Surprisingly few struck their breastwork, and the sound of the shooting was ragged, strange to his ears. Manlove risked a look. Four Apaches were in plain sight, hopping up and down, waving broken rifles. One was clutching his bloody forehead where a piece of exploded brass receiver had cut him severely.

The shooting stopped completely, and Kearn stood up. 'What the hell?' he said.

'They got the rifles we jimmied,' Manlove said exultantly. When Kearn raised his rifle, Manlove laid a hand on the hammer. 'Hold it. It'll be a sign to them. They're pulling back.'

He was right—the Apaches were withdrawing. This was a thing a man had to learn about Apaches—their religion governed everything they did. In battle, with logical odds

70

on their side, an evil omen could cause them to retreat in the belief that the gods no longer favored them.

In the complete silence, Manlove said, 'We can go any time now. They won't be back.'

'What happened?'

'Some of them picked up new rifles, back where we left Berry. When they fired their first shots, the barrels let go, or the receivers split. They took it for bad medicine and ran. Our luck, so let's not waste it.' Manlove holstered his pistol and put away the cartridges, climbed out of the pit and went for the horses. He had picketed them a good six hundred yards from their entrenchment, and found the animals still saddled, untouched.

When he led them back, he found Kearn busy breaking the branches off two short saplings. Kearn said, 'Nothing long enough here for a travois. I figured we could put these across our saddles, hooked behind the cantle and ahead of the pommel. With blankets stretched between the poles, we could carry him crossways. He'll never ride, Tim.'

'All right,' Manlove said. 'Let's get it rigged up.'

Getting Meeker aboard this cross-saddle rig was tricky business. The horses had to be hobbled close to keep them from moving. Kearn and Manlove swung up and started down to the valley, a half-day's travel away.

Finding trails where they could ride

constantly abreast was not easy. Often they had to dismount and lead slowly across the bad spots. Meeker had to be tied to the litter, for some of the descents were so steep that he was in danger of rolling off. Too, he was feverish now and thrashed about in delirium.

By late afternoon they were out of the mountains and moving across the relatively level desert floor. Kearn said, 'Maybe it would be better if we went to Berry's camp and got the wagon.'

'That'll take two days. He'll be dead by then.' Manlove waved at the shimmering desert. 'There are Mormons out there. I don't know just where, but I've heard of them. Keep an eye out for sign.'

They rode that way through the furnace-hot afternoon. Here and there they picked up almost obliterated traces of human passage in the wasteland—an uncovered wheel rut, a trampled spot where a man had stopped to relieve himself—definitely not Apache sign. At length, in the distance, they saw a huddle of buildings backed up against a butte. They veered slightly and rode on, drawing nearer as the sun went down.

They could see the place clearly now—a patch of several acres, cleverly irrigated by a spring. The house was small, neat, of sun-dried brick, a product of patience and skill.

A man came out as they rode into the darkening shadows of the yard. He was about thirty, tall, bearded, and unarmed.

'Trouble has befallen you, neighbors. Bring him right in.' He turned to the door. 'Emma! Ruth!'

Manlove and Kearn carried Meeker inside. A scatter of small children were shooed out of the way. Only when Meeker had been placed gently in a bed and the Mormon was bending over him, examining the wound, did Manlove look around.

The women were wiry and rather plain in appearance. He could not tell which the children belonged to.

The Mormon straightened and said, 'Your friend needs rest and care.'

'Yes,' Manlove said. 'And we've got to keep moving.' He glanced at Kearn. 'If we could bed down in your lean-to overnight, the two of us will ride out in the morning.'

'You're more than welcome,' the Mormon said. 'I'm Brother Spears.'

Manlove introduced himself and Kearn. 'We don't want to be a burden on you, Brother Spears, but there was nowhere to go.' He glanced at Meeker. 'We can't stay. When he's well enough to travel, give him the horse we'll leave behind. Kearn and I can ride double for a few days. We know where we can get some horses.'

'From the trouble-maker, Berry?' Spears asked.

'He's dead,' Kearn said. 'He'll never miss

73

them.'

Spears looked at the two men as if wondering what kind of guests he had.

Manlove said, 'I'm a sergeant stationed at Antlers Spring. The wounded man is an officer, Lieutenant Meeker.' He gestured at Kearn. 'He's a soldier, too.'

Spears smiled. 'Wash up. Bathe if you like. Emma, get them towels and soap. If you'll eat with us, one of my women will call you.'

'You're a friend,' Kearn said. He turned to the door, then stopped. 'I see no guns around, Mr Spears. Are you unarmed?'

'I have no guns,' Spears said, 'but I'm not unarmed.'

Kearn thought about it, nodded. 'I get your point.'

He went out, and Manlove followed with a towel and soap. At Spears' watering trough they stripped to the waist and washed. The night was sooty black and the stars were pinpoints of brightness, shedding no light.

'What did you tell him I was in the Army for?' Kearn asked.

'He felt better about it,' Manlove said. 'It's too bad you hate the Army. You'd make a passable soldier.'

One of Spears' wives came to the door and called them in to supper. The table was set for five—the children ate at a low bench before the fireplace. Manlove had expected pork and biscuits and he was surprised at the fare, its

74

variety and the quality. Thick slices of beef all but smothered the potatoes on the platter. There was a dish of steamed greens, a side dish of beans and fresh bread.

'This is a banquet,' he said. 'Do you do this well on the acreage you water?'

Spears said, 'We live well to serve God. The food gives us strength and we never want more than we have. The land grows what we need, with some to spare. This we trade for clothes or other necessities. My garden, my few cattle and poultry are enough.'

'Don't the Indians ever bother you?' Kearn said.

'What few Navahos and Piutes we see are friendly. They know we will not harm them.'

'You're close to Apache country,' Manlove said. 'I'm surprised they haven't raided you.'

'Some of our faith were killed by the Apaches,' Spears said. 'The thought occurred to me when I built at this spring that we would be attacked. We had a babe in arms, and Emma was carrying her first child. Since I bear weapons against no man, I had to call on God for wisdom. He gave me hands to do his work, and the will to serve Him, so at my forge I hammered an argument of my own against the devil. Ruth, fetch it.'

The woman got up from the table and went outside. When she came in, she was struggling with a heavy metal breastplate, designed to protect a man from shoulder to thigh.

'I have my faith,' Spears said, 'and the Apaches have theirs. I believe that God is supreme, but they place immortality on the shoulders of men of flesh. They came, and I stepped out to greet them.'

'What are those marks on the shield, Mr Spears?' Kearn asked.

'They were left by the bullets that struck me,' Spears said. 'I put the shield on under my coat, and told them to go in peace. One fired his rifle point-blank at me, and when I did not fall, many fired. Then they rode away, all except a boy, who remained some distance away. He sat on his pony and watched me while the others fled, then he too joined them. They never returned.'

'Because they thought you were a spirit,' Manlove said. He reached out and ran his hand over the metal, feeling the flakes of lead still clinging to the steel. 'Mr Spears, did you see an old man among them?'

'No, they were all young. Why?'

'The old one would be Diablito, the ghost who keeps Apache terror alive.'

'No, they were young men and a boy. I couldn't tell his age; he never came closer than two hundred yards.' He glanced at the shield. 'Many times I've thought to heat it and forge it back into a plowshare, yet I have always put it off. Some day—'

'Some day you will,' Manlove said. 'And we want to make that day come soon.'

76

After eating, Manlove and Kearn went to the lean-to and spread their blankets. Kearn said, 'Quite a man, isn't he?'

'*Mucho hombre*,' Manlove said. 'I guess Meeker will make it now. It's a strange thing, meeting a man like him. Here we are, thinking that we'd rather go without pants than a gun. He doesn't even own one, yet he gets along, probably better than we do.'

'My old man would never have understood that,' Kearn said. 'I kind of like Spears' way.' He rolled over and went to sleep.

Manlove slept until Meeker cried out. A few minutes later Spears came to the lean-to, a lantern in his hand. 'My wife had to open your friend's wound so that it would drain.'

Kearn sat up. 'Who yelled?'

'Is that just getting through to you?' Manlove asked. 'They had to open Meeker's wound so it would drain. He's going to make it, isn't he, Spears?'

'With the Lord's help.' Spears picked up the lantern. 'Breakfast will be a little after dawn.' He went back to the house.

Morning sounds woke Manlove and Kearn. They washed at the trough before going in. Paul Meeker was awake but flushed with fever. Emma Spears kept wiping his face with a damp cloth.

Meeker tried to smile when Manlove and Kearn came to his bedside.

'It must have been a long ride here,' he said.

77

'And I don't remember any of it.'

'You didn't miss much,' Kearns said.

'We'll leave you a horse,' Manlove said. 'Ride when you're able and not before. Spears will tell you when.'

'Make my report for me,' Meeker said. He reached up for Kearn's hand. 'We'll ride together another time.'

'You can bet on it,' Kearn said. 'Maybe sooner than you think.'

'Breakfast is waiting,' Spears put in. 'There's soup for you, neighbor.' He patted Meeker on the shoulder and left the room.

When Kearn and Manlove were ready to ride out, Spears insisted they take a whole ham, two loaves of bread, and some coffee. They mounted and rode off. After a few minutes they turned to look back. Spears was still in the yard. He waved. They waved in answer, and rode on.

'When this is over,' Kearn said, 'I'm going to buy something for that man and give it to him as a gift.'

'Like what?'

'A plow like I saw in one of those eastern catalogues. I'm going to buy him one of those plows with a wheel on it, and a good team of horses, and I'm going to make him a gift of them. That's what this country needs—plows, and men to walk behind them.'

'Son, you're getting religion.'

'A man has to have something,' Howard

78

said. 'Even a hard-bitten old soldier like you has to have a dream. Ain't that right?'

'It's right,' Manlove admitted and rode on to Joe Berry's camp.

CHAPTER SEVEN

When Manlove and Kearn rode in, thin, bearded and dusty, Dane was waiting for them in the yard. He called a trooper to take the horses, then led the way to his office. The two men dropped wearily into chairs. Manlove took off his hat and flogged dust from the creases of his clothing.

Dane poured two glasses of whiskey. He asked, 'Is Meeker dead?'

'No, sir,' said Manlove. 'He's wounded but he'll probably live. We left him with a Mormon family some four hundred miles north of here. When he's able, he'll come in. But Berry and his bunch are dead. We found the bones of three of the missing girls, sir.' He explained the circumstances in detail.

Dane's face went grim as he listened. 'One more item on Diablito's account,' he said. 'By the way, Kearn, the Apaches hit your father's place.'

'We know that,' Kearn said tightly. 'We saw the horses.' He hesitated, then forced out the question. 'How bad was it?'

'Your father and sister are alive. They're here on the post.'

Howard stared at him incredulously.

Manlove said, 'I could use another shot of that whiskey, sir.' He poured a glass and tossed it down. 'We figured they were dead, Captain. Diablito doesn't usually raid for horses.'

Dane smiled. 'This time there was nothing else for him to take. I was worried about Kearn and his daughter and sent a detail to bring them in. The Apaches hit the next day.' He offered Manlove a cigar. 'She's quartered around the rear of the building, in that storeroom off the old kitchen, Sergeant. Your report can wait until later.'

'Thank you.' Manlove stood up. He touched Kearn's shoulder. 'Don't forget what you wanted to tell your old man,' he said. 'And good luck in case I don't see you again before you head for Texas.' He went out.

The shed had formerly been used as a storage room; it was a tiny, dark room off the kitchen. Tim Manlove knocked, and in a moment heard Marge stir.

'Who is it?'

'Tim.'

The bolt shot back and she came into his arms. They clung together wordlessly for a moment, then Manlove pushed her inside and closed the door.

'Howard's all right,' he said. With his thumb he gently wiped tears from her eyes. 'I'm sorry the ranch was burned out, Marge. How's your father taking it?'

'He's tough, you know that. He's in the barracks. Will Howard go to see him?'

'Yes, he's man enough to make his peace,' Manlove said. He sighed. 'Marge, I'm tired.' He sat down in the room's only chair. 'We found some horses wearing the Kearn brand. The Apaches had 'em, and both of us knew then that they'd hit your place. Howard at first went kind of crazy.' He shook his head. 'I didn't. All I got was a dead feeling inside me. Marge, we're going to get out of this damned country.'

'Not until you finish your job,' she said quietly.

'Let someone else do it,' Manlove said.

'And have you hating yourself the rest of your life?' She shook her head. 'You know what you have to do, Tim. I'll stay here with dad. We'll be safe. And you'll come for me when Diablito is dead and we'll go away together.' She put her arm around his shoulders. 'Go get some rest, Tim. You look like you haven't slept for a week.'

'A day or two, anyway,' he said.

He left her and walked slowly across the yard, wondering how a man who had spent his life on a horse could be so badly worn by riding. His quarters were empty and he stretched out on the bed, not bothering to undress.

Sleep hit him like a maul. He had no sense of time passing, but when he woke up it was dark outside and Sergeant Brady was asleep on the other bunk.

Manlove got up quietly and went outside to wash. When he came back in, he found Brady lighting the lamp.

'What time is it?' Manlove asked.

'Quarter to three in the morning. Man, you can sleep.'

'I feel like I've died and been brought back to life by mistake.' He took out his razor and stropped it, worked up lather in his shaving mug. 'I suppose the captain wants to go ahead with the original plan?'

'Right,' Brady said. 'Dane thinks there's never been a better time. He wants to see you.'

'At this hour?'

'At any hour,' Brady said. 'He told me to tell you as soon as you woke up.' He turned to leave, then stopped in the doorway. 'You know what Kearn did?'

'No, what?'

'He signed up for four.'

Manlove stared at Brady. 'Enlisted? How did he get past his record?'

'Took his mother's maiden name,' Brady said. 'Chandler.' He grinned. 'The old man never batted an eye.'

'I'll bet.'

'It's a fact. Not even when old Kearn signed up himself. I guess he couldn't stand seeing the

82

kid get the best of him.'

'He's too old,' Manlove said.

'Forty-two?' Brady grinned. 'Finish your shave and don't forget the captain wants to see you.'

Manlove could understand Howard's action—the young man had a lot to prove now and was eager to get it done. But not Sam Kearn. The damned fool. Would he never learn to quit competing with his son?

Manlove dressed in clean blues and strode out of the barracks building to the main station. There was a flush of light in the east, the first hint of the coming sun. Manlove spoke to the sentry on the porch, then went into Captain Dane's office and waited.

Gray light seeped through the windows, brightening slowly. At length George Dane came in, his hair still tousled from sleep. He started to light the lamp, then thought better of it and sat down behind his desk.

'Well, Sergeant, I think we're about ready to put some salt on Diablito's tail.' He lit a cigar, offered one to Manlove. 'In the last three weeks you've given that ghost a setback for fair—he's lost his weapons supply and it's been a long time since he's lost as many men. He'll have to curtail his raiding until he builds up his strength. If it is possible, I'd like to keep in touch with the reservation and perhaps get an idea of how many young men have broken away.'

83

'If a buck goes to join Diablito, Captain, the rest will cover for him. They regard it as a sacred thing, to be in his band.'

'I know,' Dane said wearily. 'It's time we put your plan to work. We'll leave early this afternoon, and be in the hills well after dark. Meeker can assume his duties here when he gets back. In the meanwhile, Brady will have to take charge.'

'He won't like that, sir. He was counting on coming along.'

'There's no other way. I'll take Sam Kearn with us and that new recruit, ah—Chandler.'

Manlove smiled. 'I hope the captain's eyesight improves by the time we get into Diablito's country.'

'Damn it, I'd enlist John Wilkes Booth if he showed up!' He checked his watch. 'Breakfast. We'll meet here at one this afternoon. Corporal Riley will select the horses. I'll hold inspection in front of this building. Arms and ammunition will be issued then.'

Manlove went to the mess hall at the end of the troopers' barracks. Sam and Howard Kearn were there, but Howard quickly finished his meal and left. Manlove took a stool next to the old man.

'Never thought to see you in blue,' Manlove said. 'Can't you let the boy be a man without showing him you're a better one?'

'I don't know he's a man yet.'

'You're a fool,' Manlove said and began
84

eating.

With time on his hands, he thought about going to see Marge Kearn. But he knew theirs would be an unsatisfactory meeting. They needed a place to be alone, to walk, perhaps to sit under a tree and be quiet together. The time for that was not yet.

Yet she was more of a woman than he was a man, for she sought him out and they sat on a bench near the stockade wall and everyone at the station stayed out of earshot. And Manlove promised her all the things he had before felt futile and meant them all. He even said the goodbye that he had made up his mind not to say.

When Corporal Riley led the horses from the stable, Manlove knew it was time to go. He went to his quarters and found Trooper Janes there with clothes—rough canvas pants and a cotton shirt, with all the buttons removed. Instead of boots he had a pair of cheap Indian moccasins.

When he came out Dane was waiting and the others had already assembled. Brady was there, scowling because he was being left behind. Arms and ammunition were laid out and, as Dane called off the names, each man stepped forward for his issue. The rifles were new '86 Winchesters, .45–70 caliber. Each man got a seventy-round canvas bandolier to loop over his shoulder, and a fifty-round waist belt with knife and scabbard. Finally each received a cloth-covered canteen, a sack of dried meat and biscuits.

Captain Dane said, 'You may think this is damned little for a man to carry into the desert, and I agree with you, but we're taking nothing that an Apache wouldn't have. Rope bridles, and only one blanket—that's on the horse. No matches or tobacco, chewing or otherwise. I trust there are no questions at this point.'

There were none. Dane turned to Brady. 'Sergeant, try to maintain regular patrols, but don't venture too far into the mountains. Diablito's been hurt and he'll be spoiling for revenge. Act as if you were afraid to venture out too far. I want him to come to the edge of the desert, for we'll be ranging through that area and the farther we can get him away from his camp, the easier our job will be.' He offered Brady his hand. 'You got that?'

'Yes sir, but I'll trade places with any man who wants out.'

There were no takers. Dane motioned for them to mount and they struck out across the desert, the six of them riding in single file. Once, far out, Manlove turned his head and looked back. The station was a dark group of buildings and the trees near the spring seemed stunted.

There was no talking—they were cultivating the Apache habit of silence. By tomorrow they would have to think like Apaches. They would have to learn how to make a fire and cook

86

rattlesnake and Gila monster, and leave no sign behind them.

They were in the foothills at dusk. That night they settled down in a wilderness of rocks to eat and rest. Dane came over to Manlove and sat beside him.

'It would help,' Dane said, 'if a man knew where to start.'

'We may be less than thirty miles from Diablito's camp right now,' Manlove said. Dane stared at him inquiringly. 'I say that, Captain, because Diablito has raided in the valley and made it back to his camp in one day.'

'How do you know he made it back?'

'It's the way the Apache think,' Manlove said. 'They're jumpy on the move, and don't feel safe too far from their camp. I keep thinking about Lieutenant Bestor and the whipping we took in that canyon. We were close to something, Captain. Too close to Diablito.' He raised his head and looked around the dark jumble of rocks. 'If he's still after what we think he is, he's not too far away right now.'

'How about starting with that canyon, Sergeant?'

Manlove shook his head. 'It won't be that simple. Diablito probably shifted his base right after that operation. Best we can do is look for new signs.'

87

CHAPTER EIGHT

They rode again at dawn. By full daylight they stopped and dismounted at a spring. The horses were picketed in the rocks some distance away. No pins were used, so as to leave no betraying holes in the ground. Captain Dane ordered every man to strop his razor and shave without soap. They could not afford to be unshaven, for Indians have little facial hair. Shaved without soap, the dry hairs would blow away, and there would be no lather to tell a wandering Apache that a white man had paused here.

Canteens were filled, and they ate before moving on to a campsite nearly a mile from the spring—a high citadel of rock from which they could see without being seen.

Corporal Kincaid had a comment. 'We could do a lot of waiting here for nothing, Captain. Seems like moving on would be better.'

Dane shook his head. 'The Apaches are never still, Corporal. We'll see something. Now get some sleep, all of you—you'll need it. Manlove, post a guard.'

The habits of the Army years were not easy to break. Manlove caught himself posting a man at each end of the horse line. The Apaches would never do that, so he took one man off

88

and had the other sit on a rock where he could see the horses.

And because he almost made a mistake, Tim Manlove promised himself that he would watch the other men to see that they made none. Their whole plan hinged on their being able to pass for Apaches at a distance. Each man wore a headband and was tanned enough to pass for Indian. Manlove's theory was that a roaming Apache never looked too closely at his own kind, since it was impossible to move around in this country without being seen.

Since the day was to be spent in studying the surrounding terrain, with alternating guards, Manlove returned to camp. As he settled on the ground with only the horse blanket and no saddle for a pillow, he felt a tinge of respect for these savage people; they were physically hard, strong beyond belief.

Manlove rested poorly, for the day was hot. He turned vainly to seek a more comfortable position. By noon rest had become impossible—the men all lay among the rocks and looked out at the broken land. They saw nothing but a few lizards and an occasional wheeling bird. There was no sign of human life, but they knew that Apaches roamed this country. At Fort Apache, General Crook could write his dispatches east and take his bows for the wonderful San Carlos reservation and brag about the schools and the tame Apache police he had working for the government, and none of it meant a damned thing out here. This part of Apacheria was still Apache and not even Crook's Indian police dared enter it.

In late afternoon, Dane motioned them to horse. They rode northeast, toward rimrock country. They moved casually, in no apparent order, a hard thing for them after years of Army training.

Toward evening they stopped at an Apache water hole, drank and filled their canteens. Two years earlier they would not have dared use canteens, but now the Apaches all had them—either bought at the San Carlos reservation store or taken from some dead soldier.

Cold meat and hard bread was their meal. Dane talked while they ate. 'We'll spread out before dark to cover a mile-wide area here. The natural pass from the desert leads to this water hole, and if Brady brings a detail in, he'll go no farther than this. Look, and keep looking as long as there's daylight. If you see an Apache, let him through, then report here without being seen. Is that understood?'

They all nodded. Sam Kearn gnawed on a hard piece of bread, threw it away in disgust.

Manlove picked it up and handed it back. 'Eat it or grind it to nothing.'

'Go to hell,' Sam said.

'Do as he says,' Dane put in. 'Apaches don't waste anything, soldier.'

A stain came to Sam Kearn's cheeks. He blew the dirt from the bread and ate it.

'That's the kind of thing we're going to have to watch every minute,' George Dane said. 'Now find your places for tonight. Dawn is the hour Apaches like best. A few might show up here at the water hole and we'll get a chance to see what they make of our tracks.'

Corporal Riley, who was missing his cutplug, spoke up. 'And suppose we don't pass inspection, Cap'n?'

'We'll have to kill,' Dane said. 'Quietly—no shooting.' He motioned for the others to spread out but for Tim Manlove to remain behind. 'I've got to settle a matter with you now,' he said.

'All right, Captain.'

'I don't think we can use Sam Kearn. He's a man who hates to admit a mistake and you caught him in one. Another and he'll get us all killed.'

'Well, Captain, maybe he needs a little more time to—'

'I can't afford to give it to him and you know it. I'm going to send him back.'

'He ain't going to like that and he might not go.'

'Oh, I'm not going to waste a man,' Dane said. 'I've been thinking about giving Diablito a plum to pick—the Johnson place. I want him to get greedy and careless. I'll send Sam down with orders to get that family out of there and

91

take them to Antlers Spring station.'

'What if Johnson says no?'

'Sam Kearn will have to convince him, that's all. Sending him will help, because he's a friend of Johnson's. I'll give Kearn a day and a night to do the job. Sergeant Brady ought to be here with a small patrol by then. Two plums, Tim, and both ripe for the picking. If Diablito leads the raid on the Johnson place, we'll close in and cut him up on the way back. If he's foolish and splits his force, we'll let the band headed for the ranch go and attack the other. My hunch is that Diablito would go to Johnson's place and leave Brady to his right-hand man. If he does, we can kill them and let Brady take the credit for it—we're shooting government-issue ammunition too.'

Manlove said, 'I know now why I'm a sergeant and you're a commissioned officer.'

Dane started to slap Manlove on the arm, then checked himself and frowned. 'That was stupid. Apaches don't touch each other. If someone had seen that—'

'It's hard to think of everything, Captain.'

'But we've got to do it,' Dane said. 'Go on, take your position and keep a sharp watch.'

Manlove chose a flat-topped, sloping rock for his observation post. He saw Sam Kearn leave, negotiating the pass to the desert a thousand feet below.

The morning was uneventful. Then Manlove saw a dust riser on the desert, coming from the south, from Antlers Spring Station. He knew it was Brady and his detail, still far out, but working steadily toward the pass.

A little later he saw Riley moving back toward Dane's position, and knew that Riley had seen something else. Manlove left his place and worked his way back to where Dane waited. The others were there, hunkered down in what shade this stifling pocket afforded. The heat was like a physical pressure, for the sun turned the rocks to blazing oven heat. The air seemed almost too hot to breathe.

Dane said, 'Riley saw an Apache to the south—probably one of Diablito's lookouts. Likely he saw the dust from Brady's detail and went to report.' Dane paused to think. 'Brady will be here by tomorrow morning—likely he'll camp on the desert. We don't know where Diablito is, but he'll make his move either toward Brady or the Johnson place.'

Corporal Riley scratched his head. 'How the devil can you figure that, Cap'n?'

'He likes to strike at the ranches when the Army is somewhere else. He burned Kearn out while we were on patrol.'

'He did, for a fact,' Riley said. 'Sure wish I had a chew.'

Dane smiled but let it pass. 'I'm ready to assume that the lookout was the only Apache in this area, and now that he has gone back, we'll be free to move without being observed. Very well. We'll position ourselves high on

93

both sides of the pass. I think I know of a likely spot for the Apaches to jump Brady. We'll be above them, for they won't take too high a position—they like to kill, get down and strip the bodies and get out. Sergeant, take Kearn and Kincaid with you and make for the north side. Pick your spot—we're not going to wait for the Apaches to attack Brady. We'll cut them down as soon as we have them between us. If the sound of our firing carries, Diablito will think it's his men attacking Brady.'

'Suppose Diablito's in this bunch,' Howard Kearn wanted to know.

Dane laughed. 'Would any of us know him? All right, let's get our horses and get moving.'

The party split. Manlove took his two men and worked along the ridges to a place he liked—high on a sheer rock face that gave him protection, yet gave a sweeping view of the pass where it narrowed. He motioned Kearn and Kincaid to positions on either side of him. Then they waited.

For a time Manlove could see Dane's party enter the floor of the pass. Then it took a trail up the other side and disappeared. Up here, the pass was only a fissure between sheer rock walls, but farther down, boulders and rocks on both sides made excellent cover for an ambush.

Before the sun went down, Manlove caught a flash from the blade of a knife and knew that Dane was signaling from across the chasm. Manlove answered once and the flashing

94

stopped.

That night Manlove ate the last of his dry meat and bread. When the rocks began to cool, he slept fitfully, waking at the slightest sound—a bird alighting nearby or a lizard slithering across the rocks. At dawn he heard other sounds—horses approaching—and realized the sound was coming from a direction other than Brady's. It had to be made by Apaches, setting their ambush early—and since the hostiles seldom rode at night, this arrival at daybreak confirmed his earlier theory that Diablito's camp was nearby.

Talk came from below in terse, monosyllabic utterances, finally stopped altogether. The Apaches were settling down for the wait.

Full daylight built up with tantalizing slowness. Manlove strained his eyes but at first could make out no trace of the Apaches. Then he saw one, motionless, blending into the rocks and dust and sand. In time he found five altogether.

He could hear Sergeant Ike Brady approaching long before he saw him, for the cavalry gear set up an echoing racket in the gorge. At last the detail came into view—eight men in single file, alert, yet blind to their danger. Manlove levered a cartridge into the chamber of his rifle.

George Dane fired the first shot. He did not miss. As the Apache bounced and rolled clear of his cover, Brady halted his column—the men flung off and prepared to fight on foot.

Manlove was firing along with the others. He saw his target spin and fall. One Apache tried to run. A bullet brought him down with a smashed hip. He tried to drag himself, trailing his useless legs in the dust. Manlove killed him and looked for another target. He could find none—all five he had seen lay dead. Staccato fire broke out farther away, high up on the canyon's opposite lip where Dane had stationed his men—then silence filled the gorge. If there were more savages they must have decided their gods were against them and were melting away through the rocks.

Brady signaled his men to leave cover. He went up to the first Apache and rolled him over to look at his face.

Manlove, looking down, could see the dead Indian clearly; he was young, somewhere in his late twenties and Manlove supposed that back on the reservation he had a squaw and a child or two, or a sweetheart for whom he bought baubles from the agency store. In the silence following a skirmish such speculation often fleeted through his mind, though Apache domesticity was a part of life he never saw, or otherwise rarely considered. It was death that prompted him now to think about it, for in death, the hate was gone, the thirst for revenge was gone, leaving only the inert body of a man with all that he had been finished.

George Dane was gathering his men, mounting them; he turned and started down. Manlove picked up his rifle, reloaded it and recovered the spent brass. The others were doing the same. The Apaches would find nothing here to tell them what had really happened.

Kearn came to Manlove, asked, 'You think Diablito was down there?'

'I don't know,' Manlove said. 'I only saw the face of one, and he was old enough to be a brave.'

'I didn't see anything that looked like a kid with them. You don't suppose Spears made a mistake, do you?'

Corporal Kincaid hopped toward them from rock to rock, grinning widely. He went to the edge, peered down, and called, 'Hey, Ike! What'd you think of that, huh? Just like—'

Howard Kearn moved fast. He swung his rifle butt hard to Kincaid's temple. Manlove caught him and dragged him back before he collapsed over the edge.

CHAPTER NINE

Some moments later Kincaid tried to stand rigidly at attention before Captain Dane in spite of a headache and a sense of shame.

Dane sat on a rock. 'Have you any idea,

97

Kincaid, what that impetuous outburst may have cost us?'

'Yes, sir,' Kincaid said. 'I have now, sir.'

Dane stood up. 'That will be all, Private Kincaid.'

'Yes, sir,' he said, and walked dejectedly over to Manlove and Kearn. 'I lost my stripes,' he said. 'Seven years gone up in one damn fool minute.'

'You also got a free headache,' Kearn said dryly. 'It was me that hit you, if you want to do anything about it.'

'No,' Kincaid said. 'Who caught me?'

'I did,' said Manlove.

'You ought to have let me drop over the edge.'

'And have to teach the same lesson to some other lunkhead who replaced you?'

A little distance away, Dane was talking to Brady, giving him instructions for his next patrol. When he had finished, he ordered the men to get their horses. Brady's detail stripped the dead Apaches of arms and ammunition, rounded up the dead Indians' ponies and rode back toward the station.

Dane mounted his men, and they single-filed through the pass. Kearn brought up the rear, dragging a clump of dead brush at the end of his rope to erase the signs of their passage. Wind would soon do the rest. Once out of the pass, Dane swung north. By late afternoon he estimated that he had passed Diablito's trail to

98

the Johnson place. They camped before dark and studied the desert. Far out, almost blending with horizon and sky, they saw a tall column of smoke.

That was it, Manlove thought. Johnson's place was ashes now, but Johnson would build it up again. That was something the Apaches could never understand. If fire or death struck their hogans, they moved from the spot and never returned, for it meant that an evil spirit lived there.

The thought stuck in Manlove's mind and grew. After a while he went to talk to Dane about it.

Dane was stretched out on a flat rock, apparently asleep, yet he heard Manlove's step and opened his eyes.

'Sorry to bother you, Captain, but something's on my mind.'

'What is it?'

'I've got an idea, sir.'

'Yes?'

'You may think I'm crazy, Captain, but I think there's a better way of getting Diablito's outfit than killing them off one by one.'

'How?'

'Medicine,' Manlove said. 'Bad medicine for Apaches.'

Dane squinted at him thoughtfully.

Manlove hunkered down. 'You know how the Apaches are, sir. They won't go near a place where they think bad spirits live. If a man

99

went about it right, it would be easy to scare hell out of them.'

George Dane sat up and wrapped his arms around his knees. 'Keep talking.'

'What I'm thinking may sound like some kid's prank—running around at night with a bedsheet over your head. But let's say we're lucky enough to get close to their camp. We'd be outnumbered and have to wait for reinforcements. Instead we spook their horses and get the guard to talking. They might not believe him, but it would shake them up, start them worrying.'

Dane rubbed his chin. 'Maybe. Bedsheets are an item we happen to be short of, though, Sergeant.'

'A man could make a fast ride of it to the station—and it's not exactly bedsheets I have in mind.'

Dane said, 'What then?'

'I was thinking of a can of dry calcimine, something that would wash off and still be easier to carry than a sheet. And I know how to make a box kite, if we can get some sticks and paper. There's enough phosphorus and sulphur in matches to make a paint that would glow at night. Did you ever take a lucifer match, wet your fingers, draw it across them, then watch the line glow in the dark?'

'I've done that—when I had nothing better to do.' Dane smiled. 'But you might have something. We could daub a pony with calcimine and phosphorus and run him through their camp. They'd think he was a devil horse.'

'With maybe a devil rider.'

Dane's grin widened. 'I'm beginning to like this scheme of yours, Manlove. What would you want to do, mix the stuff here?'

'Better not,' said Manlove. 'Kincaid can go back, sir. He can cut the heads off matches, dissolve them and bring a bottle back.'

Dane raised an eyebrow. 'Tim, wouldn't you like to make the ride?'

'Yes sir—but I didn't want you to think I dreamed this up as an excuse to go back to Antlers Spring.'

'I know you better than that,' Dane said. 'You'll make the trip yourself. We'll hole up here until you come back, say, day after tomorrow.'

'I can be here sooner.'

George Dane smiled and stroked his mustache. 'Sergeant, don't be a fool. You've got a girl to think of.'

Manlove left at dark, despite Dane's original plan that they avoid travel except by dawn or daybreak, when the Apaches themselves were on the move. He followed the faint trails down to the desert floor. The travel was slow, difficult until midnight. Then he could move faster striking out across the flats toward the station. But he could not make it in one jump without killing the horse and broke his journey just before dawn.

He chose a spot where the brush seemed thickest, tied his horse, and stretched out on the ground. When he put his head down he could feel a vibration. A party of horsemen was passing some distance away. It could not be Brady, who was at the station. It must be Apaches. Manlove waited until it was light. He looked carefully across the desert and saw no one. He mounted and pushed on toward the station. He found the tracks less than a mile away.

Unshod hoofprints were leading toward the mountains, away from Antlers Spring. Manlove stared at them bleakly, then rode faster.

When the sun came up full, glaring across the desert, Manlove kept watching the horizon for the first sight of the station. As the distance lessened, he could make out the trees by the spring, but could not see the buildings. Then he saw that there were no buildings, only smoking rubble, with a stone chimney rising like a monument over a grave.

He restrained himself from galloping the last few miles, for he knew hurry was useless. He stopped at the spring and tied his horse there under the trees, took his rifle and went on foot toward what remained of the main building. The stone foundation and two walls were standing, but the rest was a jumble of charred, smoking timber.

Manlove found Brady dead. Others were dead, too, fallen here and there in the yard. Manlove knew what he had to do. He began to dig in the rubble, searching for Marge Kearn.

The shot took him completely by surprise. He dove for cover and crouched, rifle in hand, staring around. At length he heard a faint noise that seemed to come from the ruined stone walls. He left his hiding place and advanced with caution. He skirted the near wall, then vaulted onto the hot stones and hunched his way along.

He found Sam Kearn barricaded in a corner, holding a rifle. Looking at him, Manlove felt sick. The Apaches had blinded him, wounded him terribly in the chest and left him for dead, but some inner strength, some will beyond their calculation had kept him alive.

'Sam, it's Tim Manlove.'

He heard the old man sigh and drop his rifle. Manlove jumped down and knelt beside him. 'Sam, where is Marge?'

'Gone,' Kearn said. 'Taken.' His hand fumbled for Manlove, found his shirt and fisted there. 'Man, kill me. I'm all pain.'

There was no hope for him, Manlove knew. The bullet hole in his chest bubbled blood with every breath and, if that were not enough, his eyes were gone. For Sam a few more moments of life meant only suffering.

Tim Manlove said, 'I'll get her back, Sam. Know that.'

'I know,' Sam Kearn said. He lay back against the wall and waited. Manlove's vision blurred.

'Goodbye, Sam.'

He fired point-blank. Death was instantaneous and merciful.

Manlove dropped his rifle, sat down and wept.

After a time he got to his feet and began digging again, clearing away the debris to reach the cellar storeroom beneath Dane's office.

Enough light came through the open trap door to see by and Manlove found a large canvas bag and began to fill it. He dropped in two sides of bacon and some flour, ten cans of peaches, a dozen belts of ammunition. Then he spent an hour cutting the heads off matches and dropping the tips into a whiskey bottle. For paper he took a roll of maps and doubled them to fit the sack.

* * *

Manlove left the station, riding hard. He made the foothills in the early evening and rested for two hours, ate some cold meat, drank from his canteen, and tried to sleep. Tormented by sorrow and anger, he was glad to be on the move again. Once more he rode by night, against original plans. He followed the line of mountains, moving north. Before dawn, he started up through a fissure that was so narrow at times that he had to dismount in order to get through.

Morning found him high in the mountains, working west toward Dane's camp. He had taken a chance in using this route, but he felt sure the Apaches would be in their camp, sleeping it off. Victory was a narcotic to them and the razing of the station would hold them in camp for days, or even a week.

It was only then that Manlove thought of the Johnson girls. He pulled his horse up sharply and sat for a minute, thinking.

The fact that Sam Kearn had been at the station was proof enough that he had brought the Johnsons to Antlers Spring. Johnson was probably dead, somewhere in the rubble and the two girls—he tried to recall their names—would be with Marge in Diablito's camp.

Edith and Diane—he remembered now—two shy, sweet-faced girls, both in their teens, closely sheltered by their father.

But that was over, Manlove thought. They were women now, in some buck's hogan—perhaps Diablito's own—and maybe wishing they had stayed in the rubble at Antlers Spring.

CHAPTER TEN

So well were Dane and his detail hidden that Manlove rode into the pocket, saw no sign, and thought he had made a mistake until Dane rose and showed himself. The others gathered around while Manlove slid off the horse.

He handed the sack to Riley. 'There's some food in there. We'll have to bury the tin cans.' He looked at Dane. 'The station's gone, Captain.'

Every man stopped and looked at Manlove.

He said in a monotone, 'I didn't stop to count the dead, but the one man I found alive was Sam Kearn. He'd hung on somehow, eyes gone, body shot through. Before he died, he told me the women were taken.' Manlove blew out a long breath and sat down on a rock. 'Hurry up and eat so we can get moving.'

George Dane said gently, 'I'm still in command, Tim.'

Manlove raised his head. 'We are going to ride, aren't we?'

'No,' Dane said. 'As it happens, we only got here an hour or so ahead of you. After you left, when the Apaches didn't come back, we moved south and cut their trail after they passed through. At daylight we worked our way slowly up to Diablito's camp. We know where he holes up, Tim, but we're not attacking him no matter how you feel now.'

'Why the hell not?'

'Because we'd be outnumbered as you said—and now there's not even a chance of reinforcements. We're going to stick to the original plan.'

Manlove stared murkily for a moment. Then the anger went out of him and he nodded, turning away.

Dane called them together at dusk.

'We'll hole up here until dawn, then make a big night swing to the southwest and come in from that direction. If we are observed, we'll have to rely on our disguises—Diablito may think we are recruits from the reservation, for they would approach his camp from that direction.' He looked at each man. 'I don't think we ought to risk any more movement at night—we're lucky one of Diablito's outposts hasn't discovered us by now.' Dane's face grew grim. 'Maybe one has. I wouldn't put it past the old devil to play a little cat-and-mouse.'

At sun-break they worked south and west, traveling slowly through broken country. A wind came up, cooling the air, but it lifted dust and sand—stinging particles that buffeted their faces. The sky was overcast.

Their rests were few, but their route circuitous and it was dusk before they were hidden well in a steep, rocky canyon. By Dane's reckoning, they were only about six miles from the remote canyon and spring where Diablito had his camp. Every man in the party was a mass of aching muscle—yet there was an alertness in them, the excitement a hunter feels when he is near his quarry.

To Tim Manlove, it was the end of a long road—after this action he would leave the Army, leave a life of regimentation and enter a new, different sphere of existence. He had looked forward to a life with Marge—now he felt committed to his plans whether or not she was with him. The dreams he had built with her were stronger than habit or training.

He looked at Riley and wondered if Riley still thought of a dead wife who had been a young girl killed by the Apaches. Each Indian he killed would give Riley revenge, but what would finally be left for him? Even killing the last enemy can be a bitter thing, Manlove decided.

Dane would probably draw some post back East or in California if Diablito were eliminated. And Dane would not like the change.

Kearn sat with his back against a rock and stared at the opposite wall of the canyon. Manlove wondered what the young man would do from here on. Get a place of his own. He no longer had his father's shadow to walk in, but he would make a shadow of his own and someone, his son, some day, would have to walk in it and Manlove wondered what mistakes Kearn would make. Probably the same ones his father had.

Kincaid still brooded about losing rank. He was a professional soldier and demotion would bother him for a long time. He was a man who could hate himself and Manlove worried about him.

His speculations were idle, Manlove decided. In a day, a week, he might be dead and the others, too—and all these things would not matter at all. There was some doubt in his mind that they mattered anyway.

Clouds hid the sky and Manlove knew the night would be cool. More than likely they could expect a rainstorm.

Dane snapped his fingers for attention. 'Don't look, but there's an Apache on the rim looking at us,' he said in a low tone. 'If we all look up, he'll know we're not Apache.' He paused. 'He's taking the trail down, out of sight.'

Manlove said. 'We can't let him get too close, Captain.'

'That's right. Tim, move on down about a hundred yards. Try to intercept him. Leave your rifle here. When he rides up you'll have to get him with a knife and don't miss.'

'I won't.' Manlove laid his Winchester aside. He moved carefully in the rock cover until he found what he wanted, a nest of high boulders where the pinched trail through the canyon passed within arm's reach.

The sky was darkening rapidly. There was a

stillness in the air that made the horses nervous. Manlove could hear them where he waited. The weather was going to turn into a gully-buster, he decided. There was a rumble of thunder. Lightning tore across the sky and the hills boomed back the crashes like cannon exchanging salutes.

There was no preliminary scatter of raindrops when the storm broke. Suddenly the sky opened and a torrent descended, roaring as it pelted the rocks, and raising dust for an instant in the canyon. Then everything was wet, and the bouncing rain broke in contact with the rocks until a foot-high spray arose like thick fog.

At last Manlove saw the Apache approaching. The Indian was riding cautiously, rifle in hand.

He let the Indian draw abreast, then launched himself up and out. His moccasins skidded on the slippery rock, so that instead of carrying the Apache over and across the horse, Manlove had to drag him back over the rump.

The Apache fell hard and rolled. When he came up, his rifle swung around, and all Manlove could do was kick. His foot struck the muzzle just as the Indian was working the lever, and the gun spun out of the hostile's grasp.

Manlove knew better than to dive for it. He whipped out his knife, slung up his free arm barely in time to block the Apache's thrust. As they circled the roaring of the rain isolated them. The Apache could not retreat—Manlove blocked his way and the horse, frightened by white man's scent, had bolted toward Dane's camp. Riley and Kincaid splashed toward them and the horse reared, wheeled and came charging straight back up the canyon.

Manlove sensed that the Apache might try for the horse when it passed. He stooped suddenly, flung a handful of wet sand into the Apache's face, and leaped aside to let the horse go by.

Another burst of lightning ripped the sky apart. There was a thunderclap, and Manlove was amazed to see the horse stumble and fall.

Then the real thunder rolled overhead and Manlove realized that someone had shot the horse to keep it from going back to Diablito's camp—shot and covered the sound with thunder.

Riley and Kincaid were on the Apache while he was still trying to paw the sand out of his eyes. They plunged their knives into him and pulled them out to stab again.

The Apache was dead. Kincaid got up but Riley's knife rose and fell viciously until Manlove pulled him away.

'That's enough,' he said flatly. 'He won't get any deader. Now get him in the rocks and cover him. We don't want buzzards circling in the morning.'

111

'What about the horse?' Kincaid asked.

'I guess the captain will want him buried, too.' He turned and walked back to where Dane waited. Kearn was quieting the horses. Manlove rode one animal and led two back to where the dead pony lay.

'Shooting that beast created a problem,' Dane said. 'But not as bad a problem as we would have had if he'd gone back to Diablito's camp.'

'The rain will cover the sign,' Manlove said. Then he grinned. 'I'd have never have got that Apache alone. It makes me wonder if we're going to lick 'em at all.'

'Now don't start that,' Dane said. 'This rain's a blasted bother to Diablito, but it's a break for us. Under its cover we can move to within a mile or two of Diablito's camp and wait there for it to let up.' He looked at Tim Manlove. 'And if you're thinking about going down there alone to rescue the women, I'll tell you when. If you don't obey orders, I'll send you north to check on Paul Meeker. Someone's going to have to tell him he doesn't have a post to come back to.'

'I'm not going to bolt on you, Captain.'

'Good,' Dane said. 'We'll start as soon as possible. In the morning surely someone will go out and look for that Apache. We want to be done with our business by then.'

'Too bad we couldn't have caught that pony,' Kincaid said.

'Yes, I regretted having to shoot him. Riley, you're a light man. You ride double with Kincaid when we get close to Diablito's camp. We'll send your horse through the camp tonight, fixed up as a devil of the storm, so to speak. And if things work out, we'll catch up one of their scattered ponies for you.'

Riley laughed softly. 'A ghost horse for a ghost Apache. Cap'n, do you really think there is a Diablito at all? Nobody's seen him. I never heard a reservation Apache describe him. And I've heard some officers say that he ain't really anyone, but that Apaches kill in his name.'

'I don't believe that,' Manlove said quickly. 'We all have habits, Riley. Now you like to get drunk on payday. I expect it, allow for it. Diablito always leaves behind a sign of warped genius. His pattern is his alone. No, he's a man—a legend—but we're going to find him and take a look at him.'

'Seems to me, Sarge,' Riley said, 'that the Apaches are liable to deny whoever we find is really Diablito.'

'There has to be a mark on him,' Manlove said stubbornly. 'When we see him we'll know what it is. And we'll know who he is.'

CHAPTER ELEVEN

Those who knew Tim Manlove best called him a forward-thinking man. He had a bulldog tenacity—he stayed with an idea, worried away at it long after another man would have quit. And because he knew Manlove so well, George Dane stood and waited for him to approach. When he did, Dane smiled as though he had won a bet with himself.

'What is it, Sergeant?'

The rain had stopped. Riley and Kincaid were painting a horse and enjoying it. They put phosphorus and water around his eyes, muzzle, on his feet, mane and tail. The animal was taking on a ferocious appearance.

'Captain,' Manlove said, 'this whole thing would be a lot more effective if a man rode that pony through. You know, he might bolt and not go through the camp. Besides, if he was ridden through, he could be brought back and there would be no chance of the Apache finding out the truth about him.'

'I wondered when you were coming around to that. You mentioned a ghost rider before. I suppose you want to ride the horse?'

'Yes.'

'Think you'll see the Kearn girl?' He put his hand on Manlove's shoulder. 'Tim, I'm going to let you ride the pony through. But I'm going to see that you do it my way. Take off your clothes and give them to Kearn.'

'You mean Chandler, sir?'

'Damn it, don't get funny with me,' Dane said. 'You're riding that pony Lady Godiva style. Stark naked and daubed with the blackest mess we can find to put on you. I wouldn't smear that phosphorus on you—I hear it's poison. But painted black and riding fast at night, at least some of the Apaches may not see you. The horse will look riderless to them.'

'I expect that's an order.'

'Just as clear as you ever heard one,' Dane said. 'I'm not telling you you can't look—but there will be no attempt to pick up a woman, even if she runs in your way. Diablito's got to be convinced that he's seen a ghost, and if someone snatched up a woman, he'd know damned well it was a trick.'

'It's going to be chilly with no clothes on, Captain.'

'All right, I'll send Kincaid. I'm not going to argue with you.'

'I'm taking 'em off.' Manlove peeled out of his shirt. 'There's a tin of boot blacking in the sack,' Manlove said. Dane looked at him quizzically. Manlove shrugged. 'I found it down in the root cellar and just threw it in. No reason for doing it. And no reason for not. I just did.'

'Get it,' Dane said to Kearn. 'Tim, you

115

surprise me at times.' He scowled at Manlove. 'So you just happened to put that boot blacking in the sack, did you?'

'Well, I guess I did.'

'A peculiar thing to do, seeing that you had no intention of leaving us at the right time and charging into that camp to rescue the women—wouldn't you say so?'

'A coincidence, sir.'

'That's what I thought.' Dane turned as Kearn came up. 'Thank you—Chandler.' He pried off the lid and handed the tin to Tim Manlove.

'How am I going to get this stuff off me, sir?'

'That's your problem,' Dane said and strolled away.

When the pony was ready, they mounted and rode out, staying in the rocks and traveling slowly until they were no more than a mile from Diablito's camp.

Dane halted and told Manlove, 'Follow this ridge until it breaks into a narrow trail leading into Diablito's canyon. There's a spring down there and some stunted trees and a gorge leading north—that's your way out.'

'You want me to circle back here, Captain?'

'That would be a waste of time,' Dane said. 'Give us a little more than an hour. We'll circle the camp and meet you about a mile beyond. Good luck.'

They moved out, leaving Manlove alone in the darkness, mounted on a glowing ghost of a horse. He shivered in the cold and swore softly. The night was clear after the storm, and Manlove watched for nearly an hour by the stars.

He rode slowly, picking his way carefully to avoid being silhouetted from below and keeping a sharp lookout for the trail leading down. Dane had made no mention of a sentry but Manlove, trembling in the chill night air, did not discount the possibility that one would be posted and that the savage would be well hidden. It was even possible that Dane's earlier scouting of the ridge had been observed and the camp alerted.

He moved in the starry silence, the gorge below shrouded in inky darkness. When a sharp cry to his right broke the stillness he dug his heels hard into the flanks of his horse and sent it bounding toward the sound. Gripping its mane, Manlove swung down to cling to the left side of the animal and had a brief glimpse of an opening in the rocks just as he plunged into the murky trail. He rode recklessly, letting the horse pick its course, sliding and scrambling in the shale. From below he heard an answer to the sentry's cry and the whinnying nicker of horses—he aimed his own animal directly at the last sound.

By luck he hit the horse herd squarely, scattering the ponies in four directions. As he had guessed, the camp was in a state of semi-alertness—he glimpsed several horse-tenders among the stampeding animals but they were helpless and too startled to stop the plunging beasts. One fired a shot but the bullet went wild and then Manlove was through.

A few small cook fires were scattered through the camp—Manlove rode through these, strewing embers. A brave materialized directly in front of him at one of the fires and Manlove rode him down, the man's agonized screech fading behind him.

His wild breakthrough was over in seconds. Safely hidden in the darkness of the gorge beyond the camp, Manlove paused briefly to listen to the wild shouting behind him. Some moments later he was with Dane and the others at the head of the gorge. They rode on together and took up a new position high in the rocks above the camp.

They waited. After perhaps twenty minutes they heard the clatter of ponies' hoofs— Manlove tensed at the sound of a woman crying and Dane put a restraining hand on his arm.

'Did you see anything?' Dane asked softly.

Manlove shook his head. The sounds in the camp faded and were lost in the whisper of the Apaches' departure.

When all was still again, Dane said, 'I think it worked just about as planned—they didn't give chase, which means they're impressed. But this is just the beginning. There's only one spring north of here where they could be heading. We'll go there too—and try to get there first. They won't move far in the dark. I want those devils to think the medicine they believe in has turned bad on them. Come on, let's ride.'

'How about my damned clothes?' Manlove asked.

'We'll ride hard enough for you to keep warm.' Dane wheeled his horse.

Manlove could only curse and follow. But in a way he enjoyed his discomfort—it kept him from dwelling too hard on that lost woman's cry as the Apaches broke camp. Had it been Marge—or one of the Johnson girls?

Manlove closed his mind on the thought. Dane spared neither horses nor men and they reached the spring before dawn. It was surrounded on three sides by brush and small trees. Daylight was moments away—already the sky was growing light.

Dane said, 'Riley, I once gave you two days on stable duty for painting the Apache death sign on the station wall. If you can recall it now, paint one on that rock over there with the phosphorus. It'll barely show in daylight, but tonight it will. Hurry it up, Riley—we'll meet you on the rim. And make sure you stay in the rocks to hide your sign.'

They mounted and rode out. Shortly after dawn, Riley joined them; they settled down high on the rim.

Manlove slept. He awoke when he heard

119

sounds from the distant spring. Black figures were moving down there. He thought he saw two of the women but could not be sure.

Behind him, Dane's voice said, 'Take it easy, Tim. We're not making a move until dark. There's no point left in exposing ourselves in the daytime—they know we're after them.'

'Is that why we're camped out of rifle range?'

'No. This is just a good place to hole up. Give me time, Tim. Diablito won't like it down there—and he hasn't many places he can go.'

*   *   *

When Manlove awoke next the sun was down and long shadows were building. He looked down and saw the Apaches camped at the spring. Again he might have imagined it, but he thought he could see a woman who might have been Marge carrying brush.

Kearn was nearby. Manlove asked him, 'Do you see her?'

'I can't tell who it is,' Kearn said. His voice was strained. 'When it gets a little darker, we ought to see some action.'

'I'd like to move about three hundred yards closer and try some action with this rifle,' Manlove said.

Dane glanced at him. 'How many do you make down there, Tim?'

'Eight, maybe nine. And there may be some we haven't seen. Diablito's smart enough to

120

have staked some outposts.'

'And you think we could get them all?'

'I guess not,' Manlove said restlessly. 'I know what you're driving at. The one who got away might be Diablito and we'd never be sure.'

'That's right. When all the Apaches in these hills are dead, we'll know Diablito is dead too.' Dane looked at the sky. 'Be a good night. A few stars out.'

Darkness gathered slowly. There was a shout from below—one of the Apaches had found the death sign. A cannonball hurled into the middle of the camp could not have created more disturbance. The Apaches took little time for palaver—they simply left in a hurry, making an indistinct blur of movement on the starlit desert floor.

Dane turned and motioned his men to mount. Manlove could guess their destination—the head of the canyon where they had ambushed Diablito's men. There was a seep there—the hostiles had probably deployed near it last night after breaking camp. The seep was not enough to sustain a permanent encampment but it was water in an arid land and the Apaches often made temporary use of it. It was the only source of water left them within the protection of the mountains.

If Diablito were forced to abandon that one, there would be only one place to go—back to

121

Antlers Spring.

The Apaches would hole up for the night, probably scattering in the desert just enough to forestall ambush. Dane's men could not afford the luxury of rest. They stuck to the ridges, and the hidden slashes that ran narrowly through rocks and along sheer walls, pushing hard.

Dawn found them still forcing their tired animals through rugged terrain. Kincaid lost his horse around noon. He kicked free in time and stood cursing while the animal rolled to its death. After that, he rode double with Riley and tried not to slow the others down.

In late afternoon they hid high on the ridge above the seep and studied the ground below. A hot wind blew up the sheer face.

Dane said, 'I think it's time we flew a kite.' He held out his hand. 'Feel that wind? Like a crack in a furnace door. It'll stay that way well after dark. The gorge will be slow to cool. I'd like to have something spectacular this time. Say a tail on the kite made out of clumps of brush. As we launch it, we can set the tail afire and let it climb from clump to clump. When the string burns through, they'll fall off, one at a time, like floating fireballs.'

'We've got some phosphorus left,' Kearn said. 'Maybe a little painting on the kite wouldn't hurt.'

'It's a good idea. Sergeant, start tying the sticks together. Let me have that paper map, Riley. Trace the Apache death sign on it—

Manlove and Kearn can fill it in later with phosporus. The paper's heavy, but the wind's strong and it ought to carry nicely.' He looked up at Manlove. 'I'm going to leave you here with Kearn as soon as the Apaches show. The rest of us will go back to Antlers Spring and put our house in order.' He grinned. 'We're going to have some long overdue company.'

'Suppose Diablito goes straight to the station.'

'We'll keep him busy till you get there. Damn it, I hated duty at that bake oven, but he burned my post to the ground and I'm going to burn him down on the same spot.'

CHAPTER TWELVE

Lieutenant Meeker's powers of recuperation amazed Brother Spears. Meeker took his first step after ten days. Within two weeks he was walking around the yard. Although his wound was not completely healed, he insisted on riding out during the third week.

Brother Spears furnished Meeker with a good spare horse, plentiful supplies and a profound blessing.

Meeker was in a hurry, but he rode slowly, carefully, selecting the easy trails. He traveled in short stages, resting when he needed it, taking care not to open his healing wound, and

123

found that the exercise made him stronger. By the time he reached the edge of the southern mountains, with Antlers Spring only two days' ride away, he began to feel himself again. Hoping for a home-cooked meal and a place to sleep, he angled toward the Johnson ranch and discovered its ashes.

He arrived at Antlers Spring at midday and stopped a hundred yards away to study the destruction. Slowly, alertly, he approached the ruins. Before he entered the station yard he could smell the putrid reek of dead men.

To him fell the lot of burying such dead as he could find.

He slept little that night. Toward morning he awoke suddenly, hearing a horse snort. Meeker snatched up his rifle and took cover in the ell formed by the two remaining stockade walls. He strained his eyes in the darkness, listened with painful intensity to catch the next sound.

He heard George Dane say, 'See if you can hide the horses, Riley.'

Meeker got to his feet, dislodging rubble. He heard rifles being cocked. 'Don't shoot—it's me, Meeker.'

He left his concealment. They met in the yard near the spring. Dane threw his arms around Meeker and Kincaid laughed.

'You gave us a scare, Lieutenant. I'll help Riley with the horses, sir.'

'Mine's tied behind what's left of the stable.'

Meeker brought his heels together and saluted. 'Reporting for duty, sir, and my apologies for the delay.'

'Paul, Paul, I'm glad to see you.' With his arm still around Meeker's shoulder, Dane led him to the stone well curbing. They sat down. 'We've got Diablito on the run and worried. I expect him back here—we'll have a hot reception waiting.'

'I was afraid I'd missed everything,' Meeker said. 'Manlove, I suppose, gave you his report on the Berry affair.'

'A fine job,' Dane said. 'I haven't had the time or inclination to write a dispatch and now that we're close to the end, I think I'll wait and report to Crook personally. I want to see his damned whiskers curl when I throw it in his face that this detachment brought peace to his Apacheria.'

A flush was beginning to show in the sky. Dane stood up. 'There's a death smell here, Paul. As soon as it's light, we'll get the burial detail going.'

'I've attended to some of it, sir.'

Dane shook his head. 'Alone? A grisly business—we still have to search the rubble.'

Meeker said, 'Kincaid and Riley—are they all who're left, sir?'

'No. Manlove and Kearn are still up in the mountains. They should be here sometime late tonight.' He let out a breath. 'Manlove says there are stores in the root cellar. I believe we

can risk a fire after sun-up.' He touched
Meeker lightly on the shoulder. 'You're new to
the Army, Paul. Learn not to think of the men
who are gone. No good ever comes of looking
back.'

*   *   *

By first light of day Manlove and Kearn
worked on the kite, folding the paper carefully
over the spindly frame and securing it with
twine lacing. They watched the sun rise out of
the desert, climb into a cloudless sky and heat
shimmer above the rocks. They saw scant
movement in the waste of sand chaparral and
stone—Diablito's men were moving carefully,
deployed over a wide area, and it was
impossible to determine accurately their
eventual destination.

Neither man spoke more than was
necessary—each was concerned with his own
thoughts. Manlove was restless, impatient for
nightfall and action. His thoughts ranged
beyond the present. He found his mind
touching almost without emotion on
Diablito's purposes with Marge and the
Johnson girls—what had existed between
himself and Marge was something Diablito
could not touch or destroy, though he might
already have put an end to it. Deep down in
himself Manlove felt an emptiness, a vacuum
that might one day be filled with horror and

grief—right now his thoughts leapt over it to the ultimate destruction of the enemy.

Toward afternoon a small wind sprang up, sending dust devils dancing along the desert floor. Manlove and Kearn ate cold rations and covertly Manlove watched the younger man. Kearn's eyes, slitted against the glare, moved constantly across the desert, but there was a look in them as if he, too, were seeing beyond, to some goal Manlove could only guess at. Kearn's backtrail, which he had hated, lay in ashes behind him, but Marge was his sister and he must be thinking of her too. Still, if he felt impatience he did not show it and Manlove gave him credit.

With the sun past its zenith, heat struck the canyon wall and began to rise from the gorge. Both men felt it. Manlove took the kite, held it over the lip of the sheer drop and felt the rising current tug at the twine. He pulled it back and glanced at Kearn, who nodded.

'Should be a good night for it,' the younger man said. His voice was so quiet, so relaxed that Manlove knew his thoughts, too, went beyond this night.

'If Diablito cooperates,' Manlove said.

Toward late afternoon the small movements in the desert grew more distinct, began to congregate upon the gorge below. Though Manlove had spoken more than an hour ago, Kearn's words were an answer to his.

'Seems he's about to.'

127

Manlove said, 'They'll filter in about dusk—too late for them to make the station now by daylight. We'd better finish this thing.'

He picked up the whisky bottle with the last of the phosphorus paint in it and, with Kearn holding the kite, carefully followed Riley's tracing of the Apache death sign on the underside of the paper. He used the remaining paint on the kite's tail. Once more he tested the kite over the canyon's rim, to make sure the tail was properly weighted. The air current from below was stronger now, with the rays of the setting sun hitting the stone squarely and, satisfied, he and Kearn drew back from the lip of the gorge to wait out the last few hours.

With the deepening dusk the silence below deepened—a sure sign the Apaches were there. During the day there had been the occasional rustle of a small animal in the scrub; now all was still. Manlove crept to the rim of the gorge. The Indians had chanced no fires and jet darkness surrounded the seep. Heat still rose from the canyon wall.

He gestured to Kearn, who brought up the kite. Manlove struck a lucifer and held it to the dry sticks tied to the tail. There was enough level ground at the spot they had chosen to work the kite into the air and, caught in the updraft, it soon rose over the canyon. Manlove played out the twine; the kite with the flaming tail soared over the canyon rim, where the fitful winds made it dip and turn.

For several minutes the kite went unnoticed. Then a startled screech came from below, followed by bright bursts of rifle fire as the Apaches shot wildly up at the mocking spirit that danced in the air. The firing ceased and the sound of horses on the run drifted up as Diablito's men scattered.

Manlove let go of the kite string and he and Kearn headed for their horses.

Kearn said, his voice showing strain at last, 'We're not going to let those Apaches make the reservation.'

'They won't head for the station till daylight. We'll wait 'em out here, then follow. Diablito'll be approaching the station tomorrow night. I'd like to dig in and cut off his retreat.'

'Like cracking nuts between two stones,' Kearn said.

'It may not be that simple,' said Manlove. 'I know Dane, and he won't fort up in the ruins. It's my guess that he'll dig in near the spring and keep the Apaches from water.'

'It seems to me if the damn devils reach the ruins they'll have plenty of protection.'

'Sure, if we were going to storm the place. But when they get thirsty enough, they'll break for the spring.' He thumped Kearn on the chest. 'Army maneuvering, boy. You'll learn. I don't like this waiting myself.'

Then they mounted and started working their way down from the canyon rim. The going was slow in the darkness and it was

129

almost morning before they reached the desert floor. Manlove kept on going in broad daylight, taking a drifting circuitous course, Apache-fashion, using what cover the sand hills and rocks provided. Ahead he sensed, rather than saw, the Indians moving in the same scattered fashion.

Toward noon they began to glimpse an occasional Indian and Manlove motioned Kearn to slow down. They rested a moment in the concealment of a butte and Manlove broke out rations.

'It's my guess that Diablito will be too much in a hurry by nightfall to make the spring to spot Dane. We don't want to get mixed up in the first shooting if that's so—we look too much like Apaches.' He looked at Kearn and grinned. 'We'll have to play this by ear when we get close. All right with you?'

'I'll do what you do.'

The desert was a shimmer of heat under the sun. When Manlove and Kearn moved again, the Apaches ahead had begun to converge toward the station. As they neared Antlers Spring Diablito's hurried trail became as easy to follow as though it were a road. At last Manlove saw what he had been looking for— tracks made by the women.

He swore and searched until he felt fairly sure that he had found three sets of them—all three were alive, at least. They would not be allowed to ride, but would have to trot along,

130

probably with a lead rope around their necks.

Kearn, too, had read the sign. 'Well, they're alive, anyway.'

'It's something,' Manlove admitted.

As they drew near the ruins of Antlers Spring Kearn said, 'I don't see Dane—or any Apaches.'

'You won't,' Manlove said. 'But keep a lookout. Dane will let us know where he is somehow.'

They rode on skirting the ruins of the station. Manlove caught a movement near the spring and had time to say, 'Do as I do—' when two rifles boomed. Manlove spun off his horse. He struck hard, rolled and thrashed a moment. When he stopped, he was on his belly, facing the spring and the rubble. Risking a look, he saw Kearn down a few feet away.

'You learn fast,' he gritted. 'Don't move.'

Kearn looked puzzled, then caught on. 'Dane?' he asked.

'Right—and Diablito thinks we're dead. Too bad Dane had to give away his position but I guess he figured it was worth it.'

After a moment Kearn swore softly. 'Be nearly three hours to sundown. A man can work up a thirst in that time.'

'You'll live,' Manlove assured him. 'As soon as it's dark we can reach Dane and get our orders. Now shut up and don't move. You're dead, you know.'

'Yeah—and roasted on both sides. This sand

is hot.'

They lay motionless, cooking in the sun. Manlove had his head turned so that he could see the spring. Kearn faced the rubble.

'See anything?' Manlove asked.

'Naw. How about you?'

'Nothing.'

The last of the sun marked the beginning of relief from the heat, yet they had to wait until the darkness was full before stirring. Manlove got up and stretched his aching muscles.

A movement near him made him spin around, rifle ready. Then he saw George Dane, who chuckled and said, 'I put that bullet over your head, hoping you'd do the right thing. Come on over. We've got some full water bags.'

Their place was a pit, shallow and wide. Manlove did not see Paul Meeker at first, but Kearn did. The two men shook hands and grinned.

Dane passed a canvas water bag to Manlove, who drank his fill and gave it to Kearn. 'What have we got here, Captain?'

'Something to my liking,' Dane said. 'For a time, I was worried about being able to cover the spring and Diablito's retreat at the same time, but that no longer worries me. I watched them when they came into the station, and they have thin water bags. So far they haven't approached the spring and now that it's dark, Riley and Kincaid are at the well to see they don't use it tonight. Diablito can't go anywhere without water. Every hour he stays holed up in that rubble will lessen his chances of getting away. By morning, he can forget about going anywhere; he wouldn't last thirty miles.' Dane rubbed his hands together. 'Tim, you don't know how long I've wanted to get that devil in a bind like this.' He swept his arm in an arc toward the dark desert. 'If he goes over the wall and moves east or north, he's got forty miles for water. If he breaks to the west or south, we'll reach him with our rifles. And if we miss, he's got a day to the mountains and he won't go back to any of the springs we've doctored. Tomorrow, when the sun is hot, we may kill some Apaches.'

'What about the women, captain?'

'They'll have to go thirsty,' Dane said. 'I don't like it, but Diablito wouldn't send one to the well. And if he did, we couldn't get her before he'd put a bullet in her. My orders are to kill anyone who approaches the well.'

'You don't mean that,' Manlove said.

'I mean it, Tim. If Diablito gets his hand on a gallon of water, we'll never catch him again. It's just as clear as that to me.'

Manlove stood a moment, then said, 'All right, kill them, then!' He turned to a corner and slumped down. 'What was I ever thinking of, hoping I'd be able to have any life for myself?'

'This is our job,' Dane said. 'We bought it.

133

You buy it every four years when you re-enlist.'

'This is my last hitch,' said Manlove. 'Tomorrow or the next day—or the day after—I'm getting out.' He waved his hand abruptly. 'This is a life for animals. Now get the hell away from me while I sleep.'

CHAPTER THIRTEEN

By noon the next day, the sun hung motionless overhead like a polished ball of brass, and even for those with water, life under it was a torment. Riley and Kincaid were hunkered down by the well curbing with the stonework for protection from the Apaches in the ruins. Now and then they would lower the bucket and douse themselves with water.

Kearn, watching them, said, 'Lucky bastards.'

Diablito's men must have thought the same. They began to fire at the well curbing. The range was a hundred and seventy yards, too long for anything but a lucky shot.

In midafternoon, one of the women left the rubble and timidly showed herself. Manlove said, 'That's the younger Johnson girl—Diane, I think.'

As the girl approached the well, Kearn said, 'Captain, you wouldn't—'

'Only if I have to,' Dane said and cocked his

rifle.

The sound carried to Riley, who peered around the curbing and saw the girl walking toward him. He held a hurried consultation with Kincaid. They laid their rifles aside.

Dane asked, 'What do those damned fools think they're going to do?'

They watched Riley, Kincaid and the Johnson girl, ragged and barefoot, carrying a skin water bag. She reached the well—they could hear her crying. Then she took hold of the bucket rope.

Kincaid leaped out from behind the stonework and danced a mad jig while Apache bullets popped bombs of dust around him. He showed himself a few seconds, but it was time enough for Riley to grab the girl and haul her to safety. Then Kincaid picked up his rifle and emptied it into the rubble where black powder smoke hung, and while he was pinning the Apaches down, Riley made a dash for the pits, half carrying, half dragging the girl.

The Apaches began shooting at them but Riley and the girl were a poor target. He went headlong into the trench, throwing the girl down like a bag of oats. Meeker helped her sit up, and patted her head while she cried.

She was very young and dirty, and her bare feet were cut.

Dane said, 'Riley, I ought to bust you for a stunt like that. However, I may think twice about it and promote you.'

Riley grinned while sweat poured down his face. He picked up the water bag and drank. He took no more than a swallow, then handed the bag to the Johnson girl. 'Sorry if I treated you rough,' he said. 'Are you all right?'

'I'm fine now, thank you.'

'Got to get back to work.' Riley scrambled out of the trench. He ran back to the well curbing and picked up his rifle. There was no shooting at all from the rubble.

The silence rang a danger signal in Tim Manlove's mind. He shouldered his Winchester and waited. An Apache suddenly vaulted over a pile of debris and made a dash for the well.

Manlove said, 'He's mine,' and the Winchester bucked against his shoulder. The Apache went into a loose-bodied sprawl, lay motionless. There was no doubt that he was dead. They could see the blood welling from the bullet's exit hole in his back. 'Now I feel better,' Manlove said.

Dane asked the Johnson girl, 'Are the other women all right?'

'They're alive,' Diane Johnson answered.

Howard took her arm. 'My sister's there. Has anything happened to her?'

Diane's eyes were frightened, sad and curiously old in a child's face. 'What do you want me to tell you? That she would like to kill herself? We all wanted that.'

'What's this now?' Dane asked, and they all

136

looked toward the station.

One of the Apaches had his shirt tied to the barrel of his rifle and was waving it.

'Parley,' Manlove said. 'When he rises up, let me put a slug in him. That'll make one less of them.'

'Let's see what he wants,' Dane said. He shouted, 'All right, show yourself—what do you want?'

'Make talk.'

'All right, step out and talk.'

'No shoot?'

'If you have no gun, we won't shoot,' Dane yelled. He lowered his voice. 'Cover me. I don't trust them.' The Apache climbed over the wreckage and Dane got out of the trench.

They met at the well curbing. Watching, Manlove took the Johnson girl by the arm. 'Is that Diablito?'

'I don't want to look,' she wailed.

He would have pulled her to her feet but Meeker stopped him. 'She's had enough, Sergeant. Let her alone.'

'Is it asking too much—'

'It is,' Meeker said. 'Let go of her arm.'

Manlove released the girl, turned his attention to Dane and the Apache by the well.

He could hear Dane's voice clearly. 'Put down guns and come out. Send the women out first and you'll be taken back to the reservation for a hearing.'

'You trade women for water. Fair. Good

137

trade.'

'There will be no trading,' Dane said. 'Send the women out and surrender.'

'I take back water. Then give you women,' the Apache said.

Manlove studied the savage, a young warrior, tall, well-muscled—there were no twenty years of warfare behind him.

'That ain't Diablito,' he said softly.

'Too young,' Howard agreed. 'The captain's talking.'

'You're not going to get any water,' Dane said. 'We want the women released immediately. Do you understand? Turn them loose. Then throw down your guns and come out. You'll be given water then and taken back to the reservation.'

'Water first.'

'Water last,' Dane said. 'You heard my terms. That's all I have to say.'

'Not through. You give us water or women die. Very slow. You hear them.'

'Listen to me, Apache. Harm either of the women and you'll die here—just as a cow.'

'We die here anyway,' the Apache said. 'You give us water. We go. Not come back.'

'The talk is over.'

Dane turned and came back to the trench. He dropped into it, took off his hat and wiped the sweat from his face.

He turned to Diane Johnson. 'I know you've been through hell, miss, but I've got to ask you

138

something. You were in Diablito's camp. Describe him to me so that if he slips away again we'll know what he looks like.'

'I don't know,' the girl said softly. 'He always stayed by himself. We were always watched. But they never took me to him. Edith and Margery were both taken to his camp, but not me. I never saw him.'

'Not even when they broke camp?'

'We were always taken ahead,' she said. 'I never saw him.'

Dane glanced at Tim Manlove. 'That damned ghost—maybe he isn't alive at all.'

'He's alive,' Manlove said grimly.

'They wouldn't let us speak,' Diane Johnson said. 'They kept us apart. But my sister cried every time they brought her back. I saw her.'

Kearn asked, 'How long we going to sit here, Captain? We could rush the station.'

'And get killed doing it,' Dane said. 'No, we'll wait. He's got to come to my terms.'

'Because you want him to?' Manlove asked. 'Captain, we heard what was said out there. If he puts fire or a knife to those women, you couldn't hold us here.'

'Two of us could,' Paul Meeker said. He studied each of them. 'Captain Dane is right. We've got to finish it here. I'll shoot the legs out from under any man who tries to rush the station.'

'I'm going in after the women tonight,' Manlove said steadily. 'You want to shoot me for trying, go ahead.' He looked at Dane. 'But I don't think you will. You can't afford to lose a man.'

Dane said, 'Tim, I'm an officer. You want to pay the price for disobeying me?'

'Hell, do you think I'm figuring the price now?'

Diane Johnson touched his arm. 'I can tell you where they are,' she said. 'They're in the corner of the wall, behind that big pile of rock.'

'Thanks, honey,' Manlove said. 'I'll get her back.'

'If I let you go,' Dane growled.

'Captain, you know I'd have a better chance in there alone. Besides, Diablito will try to take the well tonight. He's got to, because he can't go another day in this heat. When he does that, he'll leave a guard with the women. We don't know how many, but the odds may not be too bad.'

'We'll see tonight.'

'I always knew you had good sense, Captain.' Manlove grinned thinly.

'We're checkmated here. We've bungled a lot of things. When the general hears about this, he'll cashier me out of the service.' Kearn tapped him on the arm and Dane swung around. There was a spiral of dust on the desert. He said, 'Dust devil.'

'Too big for that, Captain.'

Kearn was right. The base of the dust riser was too broad. It was made by mounted men,

140

and more than a few. 'If I had my damned glasses—' Dane said. Finally he reached a decision. 'Cavalry. At least a squad.'

'Maybe we won't have to wait until tonight,' said Manlove.

'I'd be happier if it were half a company,' Dane said.

Meeker spoke up. 'That's odd cavalry. Take another look, Captain.'

'That does look odd,' Dane said, studying the approaching riders. 'Their line is a little ragged.'

Howard Kearn looked, shielding his eyes with a flattened hand. 'Those ain't soldiers, they're Apaches. Hell, a good eight or nine of 'em. No dirty-shirt blue there.'

'Damn it,' Dane said. 'Of course, it's stragglers from Diablito's camp. They must have run into others coming to join him.' He scowled. 'All right, they've got to pass within range. Don't fire until I give the order. We want to make every shot count.'

'Hadn't we better bring Riley and Kincaid in from the well?' Meeker asked.

'Yes. Call them in.' Dane checked the magazine of his rifle and laid out a belt of ammunition. The two men left the well, drawing a burst of rifle fire from the ruins, and slid into the trench.

'We got company coming, huh, Captain?' Riley grinned and cocked his rifle. 'They don't know we're here, so it'll be some surprise.'

141

'They're changing direction,' Howard said, pointing as the Apaches swung to the north. 'Doggone it, do you suppose they heard the shooting just now.'

'Maybe,' Dane said. 'They're going to circle and approach from the other side, where they'll be shielded by the wall. What do you suppose Crook would do in a situation like this?'

'Have a drink of whiskey and fire one of his aides,' Manlove said. 'Captain, this doesn't change anything for me. I'm still going in tonight.'

'Not now—the odds have changed.' Dane glanced at Paul Meeker. 'If Sergeant Manlove moves to leave the trench, crack him across the head with your rifle butt.'

'How hard?' Meeker asked.

'Enough to put him to sleep.'

Manlove scowled. 'Captain, when I get out of the Army I'm going to hit you till you crawl.'

'If we get out of this, you're welcome to try but behave yourself for now. I think Diablito will attack us tonight, and I'm going to need all the firepower I can get.' He smiled. 'Be a shame if your marksmanship was spoiled by a nasty headache.'

CHAPTER FOURTEEN

Before sundown an Apache warrior with a waterbag made a dash for the spring. Paul Meeker fired once and dropped him thirty yards short of his goal.

'A man ought to know better than to try that,' Meeker said.

'He's like a kid showing off by walking a high board fence,' Dane said softly. 'But tonight we may lose our ghost if his reinforcements brought enough water for him to make his run for it.'

'Yes,' Manlove said. 'Only they outnumber us now, and we may be too tempting a plum for him to pass up.'

'That's a good point,' Dane said. 'All right, I like to think I'm smarter than that damned Apache, so let's find out. He's in a hurry to get out of here. So am I. But we have an advantage I'd like to explore. As a last resort we might swap places with the Apaches. Let them have the trench—we'll take the rubble, play it right and we can still cover the spring from the station.'

Tim Manlove grinned. 'That's the kind of talk I like to hear, Captain. Suppose I take Riley and Kearn and move out after dark and circle the station, coming in over the wall. Diablito won't leave many men behind to

143

guard the women. We'll attack the guard and you can come on in and we'll hold the station. That ought to make Diablito so blamed mad that he'll try a direct assault.'

'It's a gamble but we might try it,' Dane said. 'Get some rest. It'll be dark in a few hours and we can count on some kind of hell.' He sat down and leaned back against the wall of the trench.

Sundown brought little relief from the heat. The baked earth was still like an oven.

Kearn was to take the Johnson girl and keep her clear of the fight until Manlove, Riley and Dane moved in on the Apaches. Meeker and his man would circle from the other direction and be ready to advance on Dane's signal.

They checked their rifles. Manlove eased out of the pit, Riley and Dane following him. Darkness covered them to the well, then they began moving in a wide circle. There was no sound, until a sudden burst of rifle fire exploded in the night.

George Dane coughed heavily and sat down. He swore as Riley and Manlove grabbed him by the arms and dragged him away. They returned to the pit and lowered Dane into it. Meeker said in an awed voice, 'That stinking Apache would make a good general himself. Anyone hit in that volley?'

'Dane,' Manlove said. He knelt down, and felt the blood on Dane's chest. From the position of the wound, and the sound of

144

Dane's breathing, Manlove knew Dane was finished.

'Sorry, Captain.'

'That devil's been bad luck for me all the way,' Dane said. 'Meeker, you're in command.' He coughed. 'Pull out if you must. This has cost us enough.'

Meeker spoke softly to Tim Manlove. 'Do you still think Diablito will attack us tonight?'

'Yes.'

'That's my belief also,' Meeker said. 'All right, Kearn, take the girl and shinny up one of those trees by the spring. Be careful that you leave no marks to give you away. Get her up there where the foliage is thick and stay with her. Fire one shot, and you'll answer to me.'

'Can't I just put her up there and come back?'

'What I said was an order. Don't make me repeat it.'

'You won't have to.' Kearn took Diane Johnson's arm. 'Come on, honey. We'll put you where you're safe.' He boosted her out of the trench. The night swallowed them.

Meeker turned to the others. 'We're going to move too—dig another trench about thirty yards to the north. Captain, can you still fire a rifle?'

'If someone helped—me to my feet.'

'I'm sorry to say this, sir, but I need someone here to fire a few rounds to let Diablito think the trench is still occupied.'

'Don't apologize,' Dane said. 'I'll last that long.'

'Hell, I could stay,' Manlove said.

Meeker shook his head. 'I need you to dig.'

'You want to throw him away, that's what you're doing.'

Dane coughed. 'Let him be—a soldier, Sergeant. A good decision isn't always—an easy one. I'll stay.'

'As soon as we leave, Captain,' Meeker said, 'start firing as though you were shooting at shadows.' It was too dark to see his face, but his voice was full of regret. 'Sorry it couldn't turn out better, Captain.' He turned to the others. 'All right, get out. Go on, get to digging.'

Meeker hung back to brace George Dane against the wall. Then he left him and joined Manlove and the others. They were digging a trench in the sandy soil with their rifle butts. The boom of Dane's gun awoke echoes on the desert. He kept firing intermittently as they dug.

Then the firing stopped. 'Keep digging,' Meeker said flatly. 'Dane did his job. Now do yours.'

Their pit was deep enough to lie in when they stopped work. Meeker passed water around, then settled back. There was a deep stillness. They all listened for the slightest sound but none came.

Then Manlove put out his hand. 'Listen—I

heard something.'

Faintly, from far away, came a murmur they had lived with for years. The sound grew to that of a fully-equipped column of cavalry on the move.

'Impossible,' Meeker said. 'Absolutely impossible.'

But the column came on, driving straight for the station. The detail stopped some distance from the yard and a voice said, 'What the devil? You'd think they'd have sense enough to show a light, wouldn't you? Halloo the station! Where the blazes are they? Corporal, fetch a lantern here.'

Meeker swore, then stood up and yelled, 'Over here—to your right. Apaches have the station!'

One of the troopers had lit a lantern before Meeker spoke. An Apache fired from the rubble, aiming directly behind the lantern. The trooper gagged and swayed in the saddle, then toppled to the ground, the glass chimney of the lantern breaking.

'Over here! Over here!' Meeker yelled again. His voice was drowned out by the Apache fire. The column broke. Troopers wheeled their horses, waiting for the order to return fire.

Three men came over to the trench to investigate and almost rode into it. One went back to report. The snappish major came over and dismounted.

'What idiocy is this?' he demanded. 'Who

147

are you?' And when the lieutenant had identified himself: 'Oh, Meeker. Where's Dane?'

'Dead,' Meeker said. 'I don't know your name, sir. Sorry.'

'Spaulding. I'll take over here. Sergeant, on the double.' He stripped off his gloves. 'There've been no dispatches from this station for over a month. The old man got worried and sent us along. We cut some Apache sign and hurried. Damned lucky we did.'

The sergeant came up with a rush and saluted. Spaulding said, 'Dismount the men. Picket lines away from here. I want the station surrounded.'

'Yes, sir.' The sergeant dashed off.

'Of course I'll assume command,' Spaulding said. 'When it gets light we'll rush the station.' He peered into the night. 'It's so blasted dark a man can't see a thing. I suppose the damn savages have looted to their heart's content. Where are the rest of your men? Deployed, I hope.'

'They're dead,' Meeker said. 'The Apaches burned the station to the ground some time ago. They still have women prisoners, although we did recover one.'

'Women? Good grief, what kind of discipline have you maintained here with women on the post?'

Tim Manlove demanded, 'Major, why don't you shut your stupid face?'

148

Spaulding gasped. He ran his hands over Manlove's shoulders, trying to find a sign of rank.

'I'll save you the trouble,' Manlove said. 'I'm Sergeant Manlove, past retirement—and I was a soldier fifteen years before you got your first laundry back.'

'Meeker,' Spaulding said. 'I want this man arrested.'

'Some other time, Major. Right now I need him. And Tim, you shut up.' He faced Major Spaulding. 'The women were taken prisoner when Diablito burned out two ranches and leveled the station.'

'Diablito?' Spaulding paused. 'Have you actually cornered him?'

'Yeah, while you were checking quartermaster reports at Camp Bowie,' Manlove said.

'Damn it, Tim, I told you to shut your mouth.'

The sergeant came back and saluted. 'Sir—'

'Yes, what is it?' Spaulding said impatiently.

'Trooper Gustafson's dead, sir. Two others were wounded in that last volley, but not seriously.'

'Very well. Pass the word that we'll hold position until dawn. Make yourselves what cover you can. Then we'll attack the station dismounted.'

'You'll never make it across the yard,' Manlove said.

149

'We will not only make it across the yard,' Spaulding said, 'but we will storm what remains of the station and take prisoner the hostiles forted up there. As of now, your detail, Mr. Meeker, is relieved of all duty. I'll see that you're mentioned in my report.'

'Bless you, sir,' Manlove said sweetly.

Spaulding jabbed him with his finger. 'And I'm going to see that you get ninety days in the stockade.' He wheeled and walked back to his men. Tim Manlove stretched out in the hole.

Paul Meeker squatted down beside him. 'He'll lose men, the fool. Probably his first patrol. I remember hearing some talk about him. He's one of the hand-picked men Crook imported to teach the Indians on the reservation.'

'He ought to have stayed with his ABCs,' Manlove said.

'I've never heard you talk like this,' Meeker said. 'Tim, if he doesn't make it, I'll have to see you get that ninety days.'

'You do that, sir, and when they open the door I'll thumb my nose and say goodbye to the whole damned Army.'

Major Spaulding returned. He said, 'When the first light breaks, my bugler will blow assembly. We will follow immediately with skirmishers.'

'That will confuse the Apaches splendidly, sir,' Manlove said.

Meeker turned and hit Manlove on the jaw.

150

He said, 'His woman—the girl he wants to marry is being held by Diablito, Major. Maybe that will help you understand.'

'I understand very well,' Spaulding said. 'Mr. Meeker, I will lead the attack. By that I mean that you will completely withdraw your support.'

'Major, a little accurate fire from a prepared position—'

'Don't quote tactics to me,' Spaulding said. 'I may never have graduated from the Academy, but I can conduct a frontal assault.' He straightened up. 'We have a few hours left. Bad business, this waiting, but I suppose it's something a man never really gets used to. And, Sergeant, I'm sorry about the girl. We'll rescue her, of course.'

'If the Apaches already haven't put the knife to her,' Manlove said bitterly.

CHAPTER FIFTEEN

Manlove was awake when Spaulding's bugler blew reveille. Kearn, who had returned from hiding the girl, took off his cartridge belt and laid it out in front of him.

Meeker said, 'You heard his orders. Stay out of this.'

'I'll be the one to dig his grave,' Kearn said. 'You obey his orders.' He reached over and

151

tapped Manlove on the arm. 'I'm getting sick of this hole, ain't you?'

'Suppose I am?' Manlove asked.

'We've got fifteen minutes before daybreak. The Apaches sure as hell wouldn't expect an attack from the quarter.'

'That's enough of that talk,' Meeker said. 'I don't want to hear any more of it.' He pointed at Kearn. 'If you want to leave so badly, go and see how the Johnson girl is making out in that tree.'

Spaulding's detail was stirring and making a lot of camp noise. Manlove said, 'Riley, are you and Kincaid staying or coming along?'

'Now damn it—' Meeker began. Manlove hit him in the stomach, leaving him doubled over and gagging.

'I guess I'll go now,' Riley said. 'I don't want to be here when he can talk.'

The darkness was slowly fading to a thick gray. Manlove boosted himself out of the hole and started to run toward the well, the others following in a ragged line.

They paused at the well, hunkering down behind the stone curbing. There was no sound of movement from the rubble. Manlove glanced at the sky to the east; in another fifteen minutes a man moving around would be seen clearly enough to make a target.

A sound behind them startled them. Paul Meeker squatted down, breathing through his open mouth.

'I owe you one bellyache, Manlove,' he said.

'Did you get lonesome back there, sir?'

'Yes. Lonesome. All right, let's do it right, if we're going to do it. I'll take Kearn and Riley—skirt around and try and come over what remains of the wall. Tim, you and Kincaid come in from the side level with the wall. Let's go. Daylight won't wait.'

He left the shelter of the well, and the three men dashed in the direction of the old stable. Manlove waited until he could not see them any longer, then he nodded. He and Kincaid approached the rubble, easing around until they were lined up with one of the remaining stone walls.

With the gray of dawn thinning, Manlove could not believe they were not being watched, yet he and Kincaid reached the burned-out ruins and paused behind a pile of charred timbers. They could hear the noise from Spaulding's detail.

The bugler sounded the charge, and Spaulding led his men across the yard. They rushed on with drill-manual orderliness, like calves racing to meet the slaughterer's maul, but the Apaches held their fire. Manlove stiffened as realization struck him. 'Come on,' he said and vaulted the pile of rubble. In the wan light he advanced toward the ell of the wall and stumbled over the body of Edith Johnson. She was half sprawled over some fallen roof joists and was stiff in death, frozen into a sagging arc.

'Easy, Tim,' Kincaid said.

Frantically Manlove began to throw aside wreckage. Some of the advancing soldiers heard the noise and started to shoot.

'Cut it out, you damned fools!' Kincaid yelled.

Meeker and his men came over the wall.

'Find her,' Manlove said dully. 'She's here and I've got to find her.'

Then he saw Marge, heard her groan. He rushed to her as Major Spaulding and his detail came up. Spaulding seemed enraged because there were no Apaches to fight.

'Get a light here,' Meeker said. One of Spaulding's men handed him some matches.

Manlove started to lift Marge but she cried out and he let her down again. Her hair was matted and dirty. Dried blood stained the front of her dress. Howard Kearn fell to his knees beside Manlove and took one of her hands.

'He killed Edith first,' she said faintly. 'He stabbed me when I tried to save her.' Marge's eyes were dead when she looked at Manlove. 'He—didn't want me dead. He thinks—I may be carrying—his child.'

Manlove said through white lips, 'Quiet now. You won't carry his child. We'll get you out of here and get you well—that's the only thing that matters, hear?'

She heard him and a moist sheen came to her eyes. When she closed them, tears ran down

154

her cheeks and her fingers gripped his convulsively.

Manlove looked up to see Spaulding staring down at him. The major's eyes held an expression hard to fathom as they shifted to Marge and back to Manlove again—he was trying hard to contain outrage and a kind of shocked compassion behind a military mien.

'You heard,' Manlove said, with murder in his face.

Spaulding said steadily enough, 'All the necessary details will be attended to, Sergeant. I have a hospital orderly with my men.' He turned. 'Swanson—on the double here and bring your kit.' He bent down. 'Miss, where are the Apaches?'

'Gone,' Meeker said shortly. 'They left while you were prancing around last night.'

'Lieutenant, your attitude—'

'It's going to get worse—sir,' Meeker said.

The orderly arrived with his medical kit and a lantern. He examined Marge Kearn's wound. It was deep and had bled a lot and whether it had punctured her lung was anyone's guess. He gave her something to deaden the pain.

'Manlove,' Spaulding said, 'we'll do our best for her—including what has to be done to correct any—abuse to her. There is sufficient lumber here to construct a travois. We'll take her back to Camp Bowie. I'll put Sergeant Reed and three men on the detail.'

'I guess I'd better get Diane out of the tree,'

155

Kearn said. 'And tell her about her sister.' He turned and walked away. Dawn was brighter now—Manlove could see far out in the desert.

Marge Kearn spoke his name. He bent down and put his ear to her lips. As he listened to her faint voice, his face turned grim.

Spaulding left to organize his pursuit. He did not offer to accept Meeker's help, and Meeker did not volunteer it. He and Manlove remained with Marge Kearn while the travois was being built.

A short time later, Spaulding and most of his detail struck out across the desert in pursuit of the Apaches.

'Manlove,' Paul Meeker said, 'he'll never catch Diablito.' The sun was up and shining on Marge Kearn and Meeker stood so that he cast a shadow on her. 'I never knew disappointment could be so sharp, Tim. But then, I never counted on Diablito escaping.'

'He won't go far,' Manlove said softly. 'Marge, did they have much water?'

'Only a little,' she murmured.

Swanson came over with an Army blanket and two men to help him. 'We'll see if we can get you back, miss, and let the surgeon look at that wound. Excuse me, Sergeant. Lift her gently now—I'll slip the blanket under her.' He pushed and tugged until it suited him. 'Now a man on each of those corners. I'll take the feet.' He smiled. 'Just like a rocking chair, miss, isn't it?'

Marge Kearn bit her lip to keep from crying out as they moved her. Manlove said, 'I'll come for you at Bowie after I kill him. I promise you.'

He would have walked with her, but Meeker took his arm and held him back. 'Let her go, Tim. She hurts too much now to appreciate the attention.' He continued to hold Manlove's arm. 'What did she tell you, Tim? Anything I should know?'

'She saw Diablito.'

Meeker breathed in sharply. 'She described him?'

'Yes,' Manlove said. 'I'll know him now when he comes back here to get his water bags filled. Do you see it, sir? He'll cut out onto the desert, then circle back around this evening, fill his water bags and not soon be seen again.'

'We'll wait for him,' Meeker said. He scratched his beard. 'I guess you've earned the right to put your front rifle sight on his breastbone, but if you miss him, I want the second shot.'

'I won't miss,' Manlove said.

The hospital orderly mounted his horse. Diane Johnson was mounted double with one of the troopers and they rode off, dragging the travois. Manlove vaulted onto a heap of rubble and waved to Marge Kearn. He thought she raised her hand slightly but he could not be sure.

'Let's get dug in,' Meeker said. 'Tim, you

157

and Riley take a forward position, as far out in the rubble as you can get. Kincaid, we'll make a nest farther back and high enough so we can shoot over their heads. Let's fill our canteens and bury Captain Dane. Lord knows how long we'll have to stay here.'

Riley and Manlove worked for an hour in the hot morning sun, then settled into their shallow hole and stared out over the debris. They had a clear shot to the well and a hundred and fifty yards to each side of it.

Riley mopped sweat from his face and said, 'That damned major was riding his luck, wasn't he? If Diablito had still been at the station, we'd be burying a mess of soldiers. Likely he'll ride all day, wear out his men and horses and think he's doing just fine.'

They patiently endured the passage of the hours. The sun swung around and in the late afternoon, when it cast long shadows across the yard, Manlove saw movement out on the desert. He picked up a clod and tossed it behind him to draw Meeker's attention.

The movement was Apaches, some distance from the station. Some were mounted, some on foot. They came on, leaving one man squatting in the sand far out, like a sentinel remaining behind to cut off their back trail.

Manlove and Riley held their fire. The Apaches tied their horses among the trees and got down to walk to the well. Still Meeker did not give the signal. He waited until the first

Apache reached for the water bucket, then he fired and killed him instantly. The remaining Indians were skinned but two managed to get off their shots before rifle bullets cut them down.

In one volley, Meeker and his men had reduced Diablito's force to nothing. Two were still alive. One tried to raise his rifle. Riley shot him in the face and never looked at him again.

Meeker said, 'All right, which one is Diablito?'

Manlove shook his head. 'He's not here.' He turned and faced Meeker. 'You said he was mine, didn't you?'

'I said that, yes.'

'He's waiting out there.' He pointed to the man squatting on the sand. 'But since you get the second shot in case I miss, you'd better come along.'

Meeker turned to Riley. 'Catch up two of those ponies.'

'Never mind,' Manlove said softly. 'He'll wait for us.'

'Are you crazy?' Meeker said. Then he shrugged. 'All right, Sergeant. I'll walk it with you. But when we get within range of his rifle, we'd better separate.' He motioned to Riley. 'Get this straightened up, you and Kincaid. Major Spaulding will return by nightfall and we don't want him to think we run a sloppy post.'

'I don't feel like burying dead Indians,'

Kearn said.

'Either cover them or drag them away for the buzzards,' Meeker said. 'Dig around and find some shovels.' He turned to Manlove, who was already walking away. Meeker fed fresh cartridges into the loading gate of his rifle and hurried to catch up.

They could see the Apache on the sand, body bent slightly forward, rifle in his hands. Manlove motioned. 'Move away from me, Lieutenant.'

'We're still out of range.' As Meeker spoke Diablito fired. Sand spurted near Meeker's feet. He jumped, and dog-trotted away to the left.

Manlove sank into a sitting position and shouldered his Winchester as calmly as if he were at the rifle butts.

As fast as he could work the lever, Diablito fired. Bullets puckered the desert around Manlove. At last the sergeant squeezed off a shot. An invisible force whisked Diablito back, spun him, flung him down.

Manlove got up and walked over to join Meeker. Together they approached the still Apache. As they closed in, Meeker said, 'My God, why didn't you tell me, Tim?'

'Would you have believed it?' Manlove asked.

He stopped by the dead man and rolled him over with his foot. Diablito was an old man. A lifetime of hate had distorted his face into pure

160

ugliness.

'A pigmy,' Meeker said softly. 'A damned pigmy with withered legs.'

'That was the "boy" Spears saw,' Manlove said. 'And there're all the reasons for your ghost legends, Lieutenant. The Apaches must have driven him into the wilderness when he was a boy, and he dragged himself around the ground like a snake until he was a man. What a hell of a way for a man to live, shunned by his own people.' He turned away and started walking.

Meeker asked, 'Are you going to leave him here?'

'I don't want to touch him,' Manlove said, not looking back. 'Leave him to the coyotes and the buzzards.'

Meeker hesitated, then followed Manlove. As they approached the trees, he said, 'I know you want to let this just drop, but I can't do that, Tim. We've got to bury the ghost like you always said. Riley, Kincaid, go on out there and bring him back. He won't mind you carrying him. He's been carried for years now.'

Kincaid and Riley looked at each other, then Riley asked, 'How's that again, sir?'

'You'll understand when you see him. Go ahead, get on with it.'

CHAPTER SIXTEEN

Major Spaulding and his tired command returned to the station at dusk. He dismounted and went to the well, where he poured a bucket of water over his head. Duty compelled Lieutenant Meeker to join him there.

'A miserable damned day,' Spaulding said. 'We lost him.'

'Yes, sir, I know.'

Spaulding's head snapped around and he stared at Meeker. 'How the devil could you know?' Then he stopped, looked about the station. 'My God, you must have been attacked!'

'No, sir. We laid a trap for the Apaches, knowing they'd come back. They're dead, sir. Even Diablito.'

'The devil you say!' He looked around again, this time at Meeker's man. 'No casualties, Mr. Meeker?'

'We had casualties, Major. The men you see are all that's left of the station's garrison. Would you like to see the great Apache ghost?'

'Indeed I would. It will be something to relate to my grandchildren. Of course, you're positive this is Diablito?'

'Absolutely. One of the prisoners described him to Sergeant Manlove before leaving for Camp Bowie. Identification is positive.'

162

He led Spaulding to a canvas-covered bundle. Riley, standing guard, saluted as Spaulding stopped. 'I'm glad to see,' Spaulding said drily, 'some semblance of discipline coming to this detail.'

'Pull the cover aside, Riley,' Meeker said.

Spaulding gasped. 'Why, he's a gnome! A blasted little pigmy. Surely you're joking, Mr. Meeker? This man a leader of the Apaches?' He chuckled. 'Why, his legs are useless. He'd have to be carried or placed on horseback like a child.'

'That's exactly right, sir. They carried him like some idol of hate for all these years. His followers made their journey to his mountain stronghold to be his arms, his legs and his vengeance.'

'Fantastic,' Spaulding said. 'Wait till Crook gets my report on this.'

'Yes,' Meeker said. 'It'll cause a stir on the reservation when they know he is dead.'

'But will they know?' Spaulding said. 'He'll be a high hunk of meat by the time we reach the San Carlos. Where is your proof, Mr. Meeker?'

'We saw him. They'll know when we describe him that he is dead, though he hid himself from most eyes while he lived. Even casual prisoners never saw him—he lived apart from his men, and moved about freely only at night.'

'He must have led an incredible life,' Spaulding said, again studying the dead man's

163

face.

'Cover him up, Riley,' Meeker said. 'Major, I have a request to make. I want all your men to see him so they can gossip it around. The more reservation Apaches hear of this, the better.'

'That's sound reasoning,' Spaulding said. 'Request granted, Mr. Meeker.'

'Thank you. And now I would like to have permission to withdraw my command from this station and return to Bowie.'

Spaulding frowned. 'I see no reason for that. However, if you want to make a fast march of it, go ahead.'

'You're very understanding, Major.'

'I'm not,' Spaulding said, 'but let's say that I am. And, Mr. Meeker, if you think you are going to get that sergeant out of my reach, you are mistaken. I intend to deal with him at Camp Bowie.'

'Of course, sir.' Meeker saluted and turned away, motioning to Riley to follow him.

Kincaid picked the best of the Apache ponies while Tim Manlove got rations from Spaulding's sergeant. Since they had no other equipment to encumber them, they mounted bareback. They left the station, heading east to the mountain pass. They rode straight toward their destination, not caring now whether or not they arrived under cover of darkness.

They rode through the pass and stopped at the spring. Manlove built a fire and cooked bacon chunks. They ate, drank from the spring, and rode on into gathering darkness.

Riley found the kite, broken in its final fall. He said, 'You ought to save that, Tim.'

Manlove glanced at it and shook his head. Riley threw the broken sticks and torn paper aside. Later, when the horses were tired, they stopped in a draw, made a brush fire, curled up to it and went to sleep, leaving one man on guard. As the guard changed, the fire was renewed, and at dawn more bacon was cooked and eaten with hardbread. Then they moved on, traveling fast.

On the second day they were out of the mountains and working their way across a fertile basin where timber was plentiful and water not hard to find. The area bordered reservation land, so they turned south and rode out the afternoon. In the distance they saw two Apaches, both mounted, and they closed with them. One was an old man carrying a .22 rifle. The other was young, a year or two from Apache manhood. By the time they realized Meeker and his men were not Apaches, it was too late for them to escape.

Meeker saw the small game the boy carried. 'Is the hunting good?'

'The good days are gone,' the old Apache said.

Manlove thought he knew what the old man meant. His life must have stretched back to Mangus Colorado and Cuchillo Negro.

Manlove said, 'Our hunting has been good.

165

We have killed the Apache called Diablito.'

'He is of the wind,' the boy blurted. 'Beyond the reach of any man.'

Manlove leaned forward and spoke directly to the boy, but loudly, for the old man's benefit. 'Diablito is not of the wind. He does not reach up and touch the stars with his hands, and his gun does not shoot a bullet of fire. Diablito was a man with a child's body, whose legs were withered and could not carry him—a sick old woman who had to be lifted and carried to the place where he moved his bowels.'

He glanced suddenly at the old man and saw recognition in those ancient eyes. 'Diablito is dead,' he said. 'All of us have stood and looked at him in death.'

The old man said to the boy, 'Come, we have far to ride and your mother waits with the boiling pot empty.' He wheeled his horse and rode out. The boy looked back and shouted an Apache curse.

'Another hater growing up,' Kincaid said. 'Ain't there any end to it?'

'By the time he becomes a man who can lead,' Meeker said, 'we may have enough civilization in this country to hold them back.' He glanced at Tim Manlove. 'The old man knew you spoke the truth. It was in his eyes.'

'He'll spread the word,' Manlove said. 'Let's go. We're wasting time.'

They camped that night on reservation land,

by a small stream, where there was firewood and trees. Meeker took the first trick at guard. He sat near Manlove and they talked for an hour, keeping their voices down so they would not disturb the others.

The sound of approaching horsemen ended their talk. Manlove took his rifle and disappeared into the deep shadows of the trees, while Meeker quietly woke the others.

Two Apache policemen rode to the edge of the firelight and stopped, but did not dismount. They were an odd combination of savagery and civilization—sweatbands around their heads, Army shirts worn with the tails out, bare greasy legs glistening in the firelight. Both carried repeating rifles and wore five-pointed stars. One had corporal's chevrons.

The corporal said, 'White man not permitted on our land.'

'We're soldiers,' Meeker said. 'I'm Lieutenant Meeker, of the Antlers Spring Station. These are my men.'

'Where blue shirts?' He pointed his rifle at Meeker. 'You come with us.'

Manlove worked the lever of his Winchester. He said, 'Lower those rifles to the ground and sit quietly. Do it!'

They looked toward the sound of his voice but could not locate him accurately. They let their repeaters slide to the ground and Corporal Riley gathered them, unloaded them and tossed them aside.

'Leave,' Meeker said. 'Ride out. Tell your officers at the reservation that the killers of Diablito have granted you mercy. We do not need to kill every Apache now that the ghost is dead. He lies in the ground, his withered face no longer snarling hate, and his useless legs no longer a pain to him. Go now.'

They turned their horses and rode out and Manlove stepped from the inky shadows of the trees. He lowered the hammer of his rifle and said, 'They'll be back in three hours with help.'

'We won't be here,' Meeker said. 'Put out that fire, Kincaid, and we'll ride.'

'Crook's going to be mad as hell about this,' Manlove said. 'He likes to think his Indian police have absolute authority.' He grinned at Paul Meeker. 'Lieutenant, sometimes you lack proper respect.'

They rode southward following the river for a time, then crossing it to pick up the wagon road to Camp Bowie. Camp Bowie had originally been a stage relay station claiming a good well, cottonwoods for shade and scattered outbuildings. Time and necessity had made a military post of it.

The sentries refused to pass Meeker until the officer of the guard appeared, recognized Meeker in spite of his beard, and admitted them to the post.

'Show me a razor, a hot bath and a clean uniform,' Meeker said, dropping off his pony. 'Make that the same all around.' He glanced at

168

his men. 'Never mind rest or a meal. I want you all shaved and in blues within the half-hour.'

'The commanding officer will want you to report,' the OG said.

'Like this? Where're your manners, man? We stink. Dismiss the detail, Sergeant Manlove. A half-hour, now.'

'Yes, sir,' Manlove said and moved away with the others.

Kearn asked, 'What the hell's the rush?'

'I'm just getting the idea,' Manlove said. 'Shaved and in clean blues we'll look like different people to those Apache police.'

'That's right,' Kincaid agreed.

They bathed in the horse trough, used a whole bar of soap and made the stable sergeant angry because they frothed all the water and he had to pump the tank full again. A corporal from quartermaster issued uniforms and lent three razors—they shaved and wet their hair again, then walked over to headquarters to wait for Lieutenant Meeker.

The commanding officer had been awakened from a sound sleep to receive Meeker's report. He came grumbling across the parade, answered their salute casually and went on into the building without wondering why they were standing there at such an hour.

Crook's Apache police arrived on the post before Lieutenant Meeker returned. The Apaches had a hurried and voluble conversation with the officer of the guard.

169

Finally they approached Manlove and his friends.

'Sergeant, this corporal says they were disarmed around midnight by civilians who claimed to be soldiers.' He looked from one to the other. 'Perhaps you can shed some light on this?'

'No, sir,' Manlove said. 'I've never seen these Indians before.' He looked at Kearn and Kincaid and Riley. 'Any of you ever seen them?'

'We sure ain't.'

Lieutenant Meeker came toward the porch, his step brisk. 'What's going on here?'

The OG explained and Meeker laughed. 'Well, we can settle this. Fetch a lantern and let them have a look at us. Of course, they're mistaken. We took a different route entirely.'

An enlisted man was signaled and a lantern lighted. The Apaches stared, grunted and talked it over, but they could not make a positive identification.

Finally Meeker said, 'Well, I can't waste any more time with this. Obviously we're not the men he's looking for. So if you'll excuse me, I'll report to the commanding officer.'

The Apache police became angry, but the OG was firm. He offered them quarters and a meal and they walked away, still talking, still arguing among themselves.

Kearn said, 'I sure like that Meeker. I never really trust any man who won't pull something

170

underhanded once in a while.' He touched Manlove's arm. 'Since nobody said anything one way or another about sticking around, why don't you go on over to the dispensary? If Meeker asks where you are we'll think of something to tell him.'

Manlove was suddenly possessed with an impatience. He said, 'I kind of like an underhanded man myself,' and trotted across the yard.

CHAPTER SEVENTEEN

Colonel Phillip Armstrong commanded the post. He was a dry, humorless man, not given to displays of emotion. He listened carefully to Paul Meeker's report, took many notes and now and then asked that a point be repeated or expanded. He was thorough and precise.

'It's a blessing,' he said, 'to see this Apache matter cleaned up once and for all, although Crook will certainly raise some questions about the cost in life and property.'

'I'm of the opinion, sir, that Crook couldn't have done it any cheaper,' Meeker said. 'And now that I look back on it, I feel strongly that we were fighting a bit more than a mortal enemy. Diablito managed to embody all the spirit of his people—all their hate—in his lamed carcass.'

171

'I'm inclined to agree,' Armstrong said. 'Very well, Mr. Meeker. Complete your report in writing and have it on my desk by tomorrow. Until then you are free of duty until further notice.'

'Thank you, Colonel. They can use the rest.' Meeker saluted, left the building and walked wearily across the parade ground to the contract surgeon's office. He wanted to catch the medic before morning sick call.

The surgeon was doing some paperwork. He looked around as Meeker stepped into the office.

'I'm sorry to bother you, but I sustained a wound some time ago and although I believe it's healing nicely, I'd like to have you look at it.'

Meeker took off his shirt and the surgeon examined him, tapped him with his fingers and then said, 'The closure is complete. Does it bother you, other than being tender?'

'No,' Meeker said. He dressed. 'Tell me of the two women brought in a few days ago.'

The surgeon said, shaking his head, 'One died.'

'Oh, God,' said Meeker softly.

The surgeon filled and lit his pipe. 'Too bad. There was nothing I could do. She died because she simply wanted to die. Had there been something wrong with her—'

Meeker's head came up quickly. 'Wrong? She'd been stabbed in the chest.'

'Oh, the Kearn girl. No, she is recovering nicely. As a matter of fact, she got out of bed yesterday and walked a bit. She'd been through a particular bit of hell, but she'll be all right. It seems Diablito wanted an heir—' At Meeker's look, the surgeon broke off. 'Well, anyway, we got her all fixed up. But I was referring to the other one, the very young one. She never said a word to any of us here, just looked off into the distance or stared at the ceiling. She died the first night in her sleep.'

'Well, thank you for everything,' Meeker said, turning to the door. 'At least something will turn out right.'

'Be a surprise to me,' the surgeon said. 'Very little ever does.'

Meeker was given quarters which at one time he would have denounced as spartan. Now he voiced his appreciation to the startled orderly and sat down on a cot of luxurious softness. He removed his blouse, sidearms and boots, stretched out in blissful content and slept.

When he awoke, he found the sun setting. Day had come and gone without his being aware of it. The orderly knocked before coming in.

'Sorry to bother you, Lieutenant, but Colonel Armstrong would like to see you at headquarters.'

'All right.'

Meeker splashed water over his face before

173

he finished dressing. He supposed he had forgotten something or made some slight contradiction somewhere along the line. Armstrong had impressed him as meticulous— would probably demand a written report by morning. Meeker left the quarters and walked toward the main building, re-working in his mind the report he had already made.

Colonel Armstrong was not alone. A civilian sat in a chair by his desk, hands crossed over the knob of a gold-headed cane.

Armstrong said, 'Mr. Gabry, may I present Lieutenant Meeker, late of the Antlers Spring Station.'

'A pleasure.' Gabry uncoiled from his chair to shake hands. He wore a fine suit, a silk shirt and a diamond in his tie. Meeker decided that he was either a successful patent medicine salesman or company agent.

Cigars were passed around. Armstrong said, 'Mr. Gabry represents the Overland Stage Company. Now that he has been informed of the end of the Apache trouble, his company wishes to resume immediate operation from points east through Lordsburg and Antlers Spring. Since the necessity of maintaining Antlers Spring as a military base is ended, I am empowered to return it to the stage company.'

'Provided, of course,' Gabry said, 'we can find someone suitable to run it. A married couple, say, who are not strangers to the Territory. It could cost the company a pretty

174

penny to change personnel every ninety days because some man's wife decides she doesn't like the climate.'

'I was hoping,' Armstrong said, 'that you might know of such a couple, Meeker.'

'I think I do, Colonel. May I be excused for twenty minutes?'

He found Manlove with Marge Kearn in the infirmary. Marge was sitting up in bed and Meeker took her hand briefly.

'The surgeon says you're coming along nicely. I'm glad something is working out.' He pulled a chair around and sat down. 'Tim, there's a stage company man in the colonel's office. They want to put the Antlers Spring Station back in business and are looking for a man and wife to run it. Now you've expressed a desire to get out of the Army—and it may be that a better opportunity will never present itself.'

'This is kind of sudden,' said Manlove. 'I'd have to think it over.'

'Let me suggest that you don't take more than ten minutes. Tim, when Spaulding hits the post in a day or so, he'll charge you and bust you to private and get you ninety days in the stockade. I can arrange your discharge and retirement and get you clear of the post with all rank, pay and allowances and a good buckboard in less than two hours. Marge will be up to the trip if you take the old stage road. It's longer than through the mountains, but

175

what would be your hurry?'

Manlove glanced at Marge Kearn. 'I've never been in the stockade in my life. All right, Paul, that's a bargain. Marge, can you change your mind about leaving the country? It won't be the same as before, with no Apaches.'

'It'll be the same,' she said. 'Hot and dusty, but I really didn't want to leave it, Tim. You do what's best for us.'

Manlove grinned. 'Go tell your man he's got a station agent.'

Meeker got up and went to the door. 'I hate to do it, but I'm going to have to kick Kearn out of the Army. He enlisted under an assumed name, you know.'

'You're already beginning to think like George Dane,' Manlove said.

Meeker bowed. 'I consider that a compliment of the highest order.'

After he closed the door, Tim Manlove sat down and said, 'I had a lot of plans, Marge. You know, like moving to San Francisco and starting a business in civilization. Where do a man's plans go?'

'You've given too much to the Territory to leave now,' she said. 'So have I, and I don't really think I'd be happy anywhere else.' She reached for his hand and held it. 'The ranch belongs to Howard and me now. He'll take over and build it into something we can be proud of. Something Pa would have been proud of.'

'A man could open a store at Antlers Spring,' Manlove said. 'A saloon too, although I know you don't think much of drinking. Now that the Apache scare is over, people will be coming in from all over, and the country will grow. A man could do pretty well with a store. Nothing elaborate, you understand. Just canned goods, staples and clothing and some hardware.'

She laughed. 'You'd better get your discharge papers first, hadn't you?'

'Yes,' he said and kissed her. 'I'll be back.'

He found Lieutenant Meeker at headquarters, and met Justin Gabry, who fancied himself a judge of men and liked Tim Manlove from the first moment. Since Manlove's records had been destroyed with the Antlers Spring Station, Colonel Armstrong accepted Meeker's affadavit backing Manlove's statement of service.

The papers would be drawn up within the hour. Gabry assured the colonel that time was really of the essence. Now that Manlove was employed by the line, he would wire Prescott and have a crew of men sent down with building materials to build a proper station. This was company policy and to encourage permanent agents, the company deeded over the land in five years, the buildings in ten, then operated them on a lease basis.

Give a man something to work for—that was Gabry's motto.

Manlove returned all his uniforms except one, turned in his saddle and accoutrements. He kept his rifle and pistol.

He bought a bottle of whiskey at the sutler's and took it to Riley and Kincaid.

When he left them, they were on the road to getting drunk. By the time they were sober, he would be gone.

Justin Gabry, using his influence and the unlimited credit of his company, got Manlove a team of mules and an ambulance due for retirement. Then he mounted his splendid horse and rode out for the nearest telegraph office.

A courier from Major Spaulding arrived and reported that the main column was less than an hour out of the post. The only perceptible change this made in the routine was a quickening of effort by Lieutenant Meeker and Tim Manlove.

Two mattresses and some blankets were placed in the back of the ambulance, along with rations, water bags, and a tent. Marge Kearn was carried from the infirmary and put aboard.

Paul Meeker stripped off his glove and offered his hand to Manlove. 'It's been a good life in the main, soldier. I'll drop in at the station from time to time.' He smiled. 'And I'll send a telegram to Lordsburg. There'll be a preacher on the first stage through.'

'You think of everything,' Manlove said.

178

'Lieutenant, don't stick your neck out too far with Spaulding.'

'I won't. And Tim, I want you to do something for me. Take some of the stone from the old station and build a monument on the spot where Diablito died. Make a sign and hang it there. I don't want anyone, white or Apache, to forget that the ghost is dead.'

'I'll do that,' Manlove said. He lifted the reins. 'I leave you to your duty, sir.'

Meeker stepped back as the ambulance moved. He stood and watched as Manlove drove slowly from the post. Kincaid and Riley staggered slightly as they crossed from the barracks area, and Meeker turned as they came up and stopped.

'The Army will never be the same,' Riley said.

'He was a good man.'

'You're drunk,' Meeker said. 'Riley, you'll never be more than a corporal.'

'Aye,' he said. 'It's true.'

'I'm not even a corporal,' Kincaid said.

Meeker frowned. 'Kincaid, any difficulty you may have had with Captain Dane in my absence is unknown to me until someone tells me about it. Dane is dead. A tragedy that he took the matter to the grave with him.'

Even through the alcohol, the importance of this seeped through to Kincaid. He grinned. 'Lieutenant, you're a prince, that's what you are. A damned prince.'

Meeker went to the shade of the sutler's porch to sit and wait. He smoked a cigar and drank from a hanging water jar.

Major Spaulding's arrival was spirited. He leaped from his horse and went into headquarters with long strides. Meeker waited. When the clerk came out and headed toward him, he saved the man trouble by meeting him halfway.

'The Colonel—'

'Yes, I know,' Meeker said. 'Thank you.' He entered the building. Spaulding was furious and Armstrong was not exactly in a placid humor.

'Mr. Meeker, I'm informed that Major Spaulding has charges he wishes to place against Sergeant Manlove.' Armstrong cleared his throat. 'Were you aware of this when Manlove left the post, a civilian?'

'How could I be, sir? Major Spaulding had not yet arrived.'

'Blast it!' Spaulding roared. 'You heard me promise Manlove ninety days in the guardhouse.'

'I did, but I didn't take you seriously, sir, for I've promised men that myself and had no intention of following through.' Meeker smiled. 'Besides, sir, you were excited and overwrought.'

'Me? Excited? Overwrought?' Spaulding threw his kepi to the floor and flung himself into a chair.

'I think we've heard enough,' Armstrong said. 'Really, Spaulding, you can't expect me to recall the man, reenlist him just so you can charge him.'

'Blast it, then I'll charge his commanding officer.' Spaulding stabbed a finger at Meeker.

'That will be awkward,' Armstrong said. 'I've mentioned Meeker favorably in my report to Crook. Matter of fact, I recommended a promotion.' He got up from his desk and went around to put a hand on Spaulding's shoulder. 'We'll talk about this later, after you've had a chance to consider it all in proper perspective.' His glance came up and touched Paul Meeker's. 'You're excused, Mr. Meeker.'

On the porch, Meeker paused, breathed deeply, then started to whistle.

A promotion would not be bad. Silver bars at twenty-four. Of course it would mean a company command, a chance to distinguish himself. His thoughts remained on the future, his future in the Army, and things outside that sphere did not come into his mind at all.

*　　*　　*

Manlove and Howard Kearn helped Marge from the wagon at their night camp along the stage road. Kearn built the fire while Manlove chopped wood for the night. Then Kearn began to fidget.

Manlove asked, 'Are we traveling too slow

181

for you?'

'Seems like I can't get home fast enough. Funny—all I wanted to do was get away—now I want to get back, start fixing the place up.' He laughed and sat down by the fire. 'Tim, let's build that monument first.'

'How did you know about that?'

'Paul mentioned it. I want to make it big so it can be seen for miles. I don't want anyone, Apache or white, to forget what it cost.'

'We'll build it,' Manlove said quietly. 'But they'll forget, just the same. Let's fry some bacon.'

We hope you have enjoyed this Large Print book. Other Chivers Press or G. K. Hall Large Print books are available at your library or directly from the publishers. For more information about current and forthcoming titles, please call or write, without obligation, to:

Chivers Press Limited
Windsor Bridge Road
Bath BA2 3AX
England
Tel. (01225) 335336

OR

G. K. Hall
P.O. Box 159
Thorndike, Maine 04986
USA
Tel. (800) 223–6121 (U.S. & Canada)
In Maine call collect: (207) 948–2962

All our Large Print titles are designed for easy reading, and all our books are made to last.

Will Cook is the author of numerous outstanding Western novels as well as historical frontier fiction. He was born in Richmond, Indiana, but was raised by an aunt and uncle in Cambridge, Illinois. He joined the U.S. cavalry at the age of sixteen but was disillusioned because horses were being eliminated through mechanization. He transferred to the U.S. Army Air Force in which he served in the South Pacific during the Second World War. Cook turned to writing in 1951 and contributed a number of outstanding short stories to DIME WESTERN and other pulp magazines as well as fiction for major smooth-paper magazines such as THE SATURDAY EVENING POST. It was in the POST that his best-known novel COMANCHE CAPTIVES was serialized. It was later filmed as TWO RODE TOGETHER (Columbia, 1961) directed by John Ford and starring James Stewart and Richard Widmark. Sometimes in his short stories Cook would introduce characters that would later be featured in novels, such as Charlie Boomhauer who first appeared in 'Lawmen Die Sudden' in BIG-BOOK WESTERN in 1953 and is later to be found in BADMAN'S HOLIDAY (1958) and THE WIND RIVER KID (1958). Along with his steady productivity, Cook maintained an enviable quality. His novels range widely in time and place, from the Illinois frontier of 1811 to southwest Texas in 1905, but each is peopled with credible and interesting characters whose interactions form the backbone of the narrative. Most of his novels deal with more or less traditional Western themes—range wars, reformed outlaws, cattle rustling, Indian fighting—but there are also romantic novels such as SABRINA KANE (1956) and exercises in historical realism such as ELIZABETH, BY NAME (1958). Indeed, his fiction is known for its strong heroines. Another common feature is Cook's compassion for his characters who must be able to survive in a wild and violent land. His protagonists make mistakes, hurt people they care for, and sometimes succumb to ignoble impulses, but this all provides an added dimension to the artistry of his work.